I0731445

FRESHWATER KISSES

KRISTA LAKES

ZIRCONIA PUBLISHING, INC.

ABOUT THIS BOOK

Everything in Samantha Conners' life seemed to be in a holding pattern. Her sailboat racing season had fallen through, and she was stuck in a dead end job that barely covered the bills. If it wasn't for the fact that her sister and niece were depending on her, she would have never been out on the water the day the billionaire's boat ran her over.

Robbie Saunders is convinced that he is the screw-up younger brother of billionaire Jack Saunders. One of his biggest rules was to never go out drunk on the water, but with the impending death of his father, he took the boat out after drinking to try and gain some clarity. Instead, he ran over Sam and barely managed to save her from drowning.

While the two had been childhood sweethearts, time and distance had made them into different people. When fate crashed them back together, Robbie finds the fiery young woman to be the person he needs to give him motivation and direction. For Sam, Robbie is growing into the man she always knew he could be. A love blossoms and grows.

But what fate can give, it can also take away. A storm during the biggest freshwater sailing race of Sam's career changes everything. Will Sam and Robbie find a way to overcome the storm, or will the two only have memories of freshwater kisses?

The ocean was as warm as bathwater. I surfaced, kicking water at him. He raised his arm to block the spray, but then roared and started swimming for me. I shrieked and swam away, kicking my legs and swinging my arms as he chased me through the warm waves.

Robbie was always the faster swimmer, and it was only a matter of minutes before he finally caught me by the aft of the ship. His hand wrapped around my ankle and he dunked me under with a swift downward pull. I shook my head free of the water as I emerged, opening my eyes to find him close enough to kiss. The moonlight caught the gleam in his eye as he pulled me closer to him, holding onto the boat to keep us both afloat.

"Kiss me," I said with just a hint of begging. I licked the salt from my lips. His mouth curved up into a smile and he tipped his head to the side, bringing his lips to mine. His tongue was salty with the ocean water as he tasted me, our lips dancing in the dark. Heat began to burn in my core. I didn't want to wait any longer. I wanted Robbie more than I wanted to breathe...

Don't forget to sign up for <u>my newsletter</u>! You'll be the first to see my new covers, comment on new books of mine, and always know when books are available for free or on sale!

CHAPTER 1

Eleven Years Ago...

The bright sunshine sparkled on the blue water, turning the sea into a giant twinkling gemstone; the waves shushed against our small boat in loving caresses, begging us to stay out on the ocean just a little longer. I wanted to stay out on the water with Robbie forever. Today was my last day with my best friend.

I played with the end of a rope, hoping that the day would just freeze and that I wouldn't have to leave. My dad had quit his job with DS Oil and Gas to start out on his own and now we were having to move. I didn't understand why he wanted to quit; things were good the way they were. I was happy. I liked my middle school, I liked this neighborhood, but mostly, I liked being with my best friend. Moving was going to take all of it away.

The other boats from our sailing class were already tied at the docks and the students and instructors were getting ready to go home. Robbie and I sat out in our sailboat, sails down and bobbing gently on the waves, pretending that the class wasn't over yet. Our instructor, Mr. Henderson, was still out on the water in the boat next to us, but he understood why Robbie and I didn't want to go back to shore. This was the last time we were going to sail together. Mr. Henderson just sat in his small dinghy, pretending not to see us dawdling. There was a reason he was my favorite teacher.

"Hey, Robbie, come here! You have got to see this fish!" I cried out, peering down at the water. There was no fish, but I knew Robbie couldn't resist. He fell for this every time.

"Really? Coming!" Robbie hurried over, his skinny frame brushing against mine as he came to see what I was looking at. As soon as he leaned over the edge, I gave his shoulders a strong push, and he toppled into the blue water with a yell.

"Yup, it's a Robbie-fish!" I yelled, laughing as he surfaced. He sputtered and wiped the water out of his green eyes. He made a face at me and started swimming to the rear of the boat where he could climb back up. Our boat was a simple two-person sailboat. It didn't have a motor and was just the right size to teach two kids how to sail.

"Hey, help me up," he called from the side of the boat. I knew what was coming, but I reached my hand out toward his. This was tradition with us. Our hands met, his hand cold and wet as he wrapped his fingers around my wrist. His small arms yanked down hard; Robbie was much stronger than he looked, and he easily toppled me off the boat and into the water.

The cold water made me gasp; my mouth filling with cold, salty brine. I surfaced and wiped my eyes, spitting out a mouthful of ocean at Robbie's face. The two of us looked at one another and giggled. As we tread water, he splashed me and I splashed him back. I loved this; I didn't want it to end.

"Come on, you two, it's time to head back in," Mr. Henderson called. I sighed. Robbie lifted himself out of the water and into the boat. I followed, wringing the water out of my blonde ponytail, and leaving a trail of water across the deck.

Robbie raised the mainsail, keeping the smaller jib sails down. It was easier to manage the tricky maneuver into the dock with only one sail to worry about. I took the tiller and began steering the boat back to shore.

The wind was just right to sail smoothly into the wooden dock. Robbie had the dock lines ready and he jumped easily to the dock and tied up the boat. I started bringing down the sail and tying everything up to prepare the boat for the night. Our instructor sailed in easily behind us, Robbie catching his ropes and tying him to the dock as well.

"Good job, you two," Mr. Henderson praised as he watched us carefully. "Pop quiz: Sam, what are the names of the sails and what do they do?"

"The sails are the mainsail and the jib. The mainsail is the big sail that gives most of the power and the jib is the smaller sail in front that increases speed and improves handling," I answered.

"Very good. Now, Robbie, tell me about rigging and sheets."

Robbie finished tying off one of the ropes that held the instructor's dinghy to the dock before standing and answering.

"The rigging is the cables and ropes that support the mast and sails. The lines that control the sails are called sheets, and they are held in place by cleats and winches. You use a winch to tighten the sheet to trim, or adjust and position the sails to go faster." It would have been the perfect answer, if his voice hadn't cracked, dropping him from boyish soprano to a manly bass mid-sentence. I managed to keep the smile off my face since I knew he hated when that happened. Robbie ran his hand through his hair, sending little water droplets flying through the air as he tried to look nonchalant about it.

The instructor gave us both a big smile, completely ignoring Robbie's puberty crisis. "Very good, you two. Everything looks all tied up here. Good job today." He paused and put his hands on my shoulders. "Sam, I'm sorry that this is our last class together. You are an amazing sailor and I'm so glad I got to have you as a student. Keep at it, and I'll be cheering for you at the Olympics in a few years."

I leaned forward and gave him a hug, feeling my wet clothes soaking his dry ones. He hugged me back before letting go.

"I'll see you next week, Robbie. Sam, good luck with everything," he said as he pulled away. He gave us both smiles and turned and walked away. I watched him go down the dock like I had after every sailing lesson, but today I felt my heart sink because it was my last lesson. As soon as my dad arrived to take me away, this would all be over. Now that I was off the boat, the fact that I was leaving was suddenly very real.

Robbie must have sensed my sadness, so he grabbed my hand and pulled me down the dock. "Come on, let's go rinse off," he said. His hand was warm in mine, and I hoped he wouldn't let go. He was my best friend. We had been paired up as sailing partners when we first started sailing, and now, I didn't want to sail with anyone else. I didn't want to leave and have to start over. I wished again that Dad wasn't quitting his job. This sucked.

At the end of the dock was a small spigot with a banged-up white bucket next to it. Robbie let go of my hand and turned it on, filling the bucket with freshwater. I watched the clear liquid sparkle in the afternoon sun as it filled the pail. It seemed to take forever, but I was glad. I wanted to stay here forever. I wanted to stay with Robbie.

"Do you have a house in Texas yet?" Robbie asked. His eyes stayed on the bucket, watching it fill up slowly. Our hands had found their way back together again.

"No. He's not even sure if we'll actually end up there. I don't know why he can't just keep working for your dad. He says he's wanted to start his own company for a long time and this is the best opportunity, but... I don't care. I don't want to move," I said. Robbie squeezed my hand.

"My dad doesn't want yours to go, but there isn't anything he can do about it. You promise you'll keep in touch? Maybe you can come back to New York for Christmas or something?" Hope raised Robbie's voice an octave.

"I hope so. That would be great." It was my turn to squeeze Robbie's hand. "I'm going to miss you."

"Me too," he said softly. There was a note of hurt in his voice that made me feel even more awful. Despite being a billionaire's son, Robbie didn't have a lot of friends. It was usually just him and me. Sometimes Gavin would join us, and we'd be the Three Musketeers, but Gavin didn't like to sail. Robbie and I lived for sailing. I wasn't sure what I was going to do without him.

Robbie turned off the water, and then dipped a finger into the bucket to test the temperature.

"It's warm today," he said, turning to me with a grin.

Some days it was ice cold, but the sun had been shining all day. Warm was always better.

A car's brakes squeaked in the parking lot, and I saw my father's black Mercedes pulling into a parking space. We didn't have much time. Robbie saw it too, and so he lifted the bucket over our heads. We would just have to share the bucket this time, pouring it over both of us to rinse off the salt.

I stepped in close to him, feeling my heart start to beat faster. I didn't know why, but being around Robbie recently made my heart start to pound. He was my best friend, but I could feel my body starting to ask for more. I wondered if he felt the same way.

Robbie steadied the bucket and then slowly tipped it over to cascade the water down over the two of us. I moved without thinking, leaning forward and kissing him on the lips. The water sparkled around us in the sunshine as I pressed my mouth against his.

Robbie froze. The bucket fell from his hands with a clatter. My father's voice called my name, and I gave Robbie a hug, squeezing my eyes shut tight. I didn't want to let him go, but I knew I had to. He wrapped his arms around me and squeezed back, holding me like he was never going to let go.

"Samantha? It's time to leave," my father called from the car. I had to go. Robbie's arms slowly released me, and I stepped back. There were tears in his green eyes.

"Bye, Robbie," I whispered and darted away as fast as I could. I didn't want him to see me cry.

I ran to the car, leaving a trail of wet footprints behind me. My dad was standing in the open door of his car, resting his arms on the frame as he waited for me. I knew there would be dry towels in the back seat for me to sit on.

I slammed the door shut, wrapping a towel around me like a blanket. I wiped at my nose, feeling the tears trickle down my face. Dad's door closed, and he backed out of the parking lot. He stayed quiet, letting me have a moment alone. Through the window I could still see Robbie standing there, the bucket rolling gently at his feet.

The car backed out, and I pressed a hand to the glass to wave goodbye. Robbie mirrored my gesture, raising his hand toward me. The car turned down the street, and Robbie was gone.

CHAPTER 2

I pulled into the driveway and turned off the engine. It was a cute little house, quaint with a big white door. It looked like something a grandmother would live in, which was appropriate because Betty lived here, my niece's grandmother. Or rather, she had lived here.

Sighing as I leaned back in the truck's seat, I still couldn't believe I was here, but family has to stick together. My sister, Grace, needed me. When she called to tell me Betty had died, I packed my truck the next day. Grace wouldn't officially ask me to move in, but Grace was going to have a rough time without Betty's help watching her daughter.

Five years old and one of the smartest little kids I had ever met, Avery was incredibly independent and a total handful. It wasn't that she misbehaved; but just like her dad, she was too smart for her own good and she had an impulsive spirit, just like her father. Often, she didn't think before she acted.

I wondered how well Grace was holding up. She was strong, but I was sure Betty's death was taking its toll on her.

She had already lost so much; the death of one more person close to her seemed cruel. Our parents died when I was fifteen and Grace was nineteen. She had petitioned the courts and taken legal guardianship of me. It was just us; two teenage girls taking on the world. But, together, we survived.

The truck groaned slightly as it settled. I closed my eyes, thinking back on how things had been and how we got to this point.

Grace and her boyfriend, Evan, finished raising me after Mom and Dad died. I had been excited when Grace told Evan she was pregnant a year after the three of us had moved in together. I was sixteen at the time and thought having a baby around the house would be fun. Evan joined the Army so that he could support his growing family, and he married Grace in a simple ceremony in front of an Army chaplain before Avery was born. Money was tight, but we were happy. We were a family.

Evan worked so hard to keep Grace, Avery, and me comfortable. We were "his girls," and we traveled from base to base across the country wherever the Army sent him. Things were good, the future looked bright. Then I came home one day to find a man in uniform with a flag tucked under his arm and an apologetic look on his face. Evan's impulsive spirit had cost him dearly. The Army chaplain said he didn't even hesitate to run into the fire and had saved three lives because of it. Avery was only three.

After Evan died, his mother, Betty, asked Grace and Avery to come live with her. I had a sailing scholarship waiting for me in California, so I went off to school while Grace and Avery moved back to the East Coast. I visited as often as I could, but even with my sailing competitions occasionally sending me back East, I only saw them at Christmas and spring break. I missed them, but my sailing career was taking off. *Well*, I thought, *it* had *been.*

Without air conditioning, the truck's cabin started to heat up. It was still early summer, but the late afternoon sun beat through the windshield. It felt almost good in a drowsy sort of way, but I knew before long it would become unbearable. I was rather excited, looking forward to a shower and a night in a real bed. Traveling cross-country in an old beat-up pickup with barely enough money to pay for gas, let alone a decent hotel, made for some uncomfortable nights stretched out across the passenger seat.

A little face framed with dark blonde hair appeared in the front window of the house, as I turned into the driveway and shut off the car. Blue eyes peered out at me and a huge grin spread across her face when I waved. My time in the driveway was over. Even from the car, I could hear her little voice shouting, "AUNT SAM'S HERE! MOM! AUNT SAM'S HERE!"

The old truck's door gave a metallic sigh when I opened it, and I stretched as soon as I could stand. My butt was numb from sitting for so long. The slight breeze was cool after being in the car, and it felt amazing. Even though we were at least a mile inland, I could almost smell the ocean. One upside to moving here was a fantastic little marina just a mile away. Not that I had a boat or anyone to sail it with, but at least it was there.

The front door of the house made a thud against the wall after Avery threw it open and ran screaming joyfully into the driveway. Kneeling just in time to have her little arms slam around my neck, she giggled with delight as I squeezed her back. I held her at arm's length and looked her up and down.

"Hmm, maybe you know where I can find my niece," I

said with a fake frown. "She looks a lot like you, but she isn't nearly as tall. And my niece is definitely cleaner." Spaghetti sauce streaked Avery's face, and I was fairly sure that was glitter glue in her hair. Her shirt, and now mine, was covered in flour. I could just bet that her mom was eager for the little monster to start school in a couple months.

"It's me, Aunt Sam! Mom and I made cookies!" Avery grinned proudly. "And I lost a tooth yesterday and the Tooth Fairy gave me a whole dollar! And Mom said that we can go to the store later and I can buy something, and..."

"Let your aunt breathe, Avery. You can tell her your life story once we get her inside," Grace said, interrupting the stream of bubbly words coming from the excited five year old. "I thought you weren't going to be here until tomorrow?"

I stood up and gave my sister a hug. Her blue eyes were tired with dark circles underneath, but she still grinned and firmly returned my hug. I wondered just how much sleep she had, or hadn't, been getting.

"I got woken up at the rest stop by some guy's car alarm going off at two in the morning, so I just got on the road early," I said. "Avery mentioned something about cookies?"

Grace's laugh brightened her features.

Avery grabbed my hand. "We made chocolate chip, and sugar, and Mom let me decorate them, and..."

"And I'm guessing she let you eat a couple of them too," I butted in. Avery gave me a toothy grin as she pulled me into the door. The house was cool and comfortable. It was just the way I remembered it from my last visit.

I sat down at the worn, wooden kitchen table while Avery chattered on about how she had decorated this cookie and that cookie. Grace poured me a tall glass of lemonade that I slowly sipped. She frowned slightly at a knock on the door, but before she could move, Avery sprinted to answer it.

"Avery, remember to look out the window before..." Grace called out as the door pinged against the wall again. "Before you answer it." Grace sighed, I set down my drink, and together we followed the chatter to the front door.

A big man in a sheriff's uniform was in the doorway, already down on one knee and listening to Avery's barrage of words. He was at least twenty years older than Grace and me, but he had a kind face. Rising as soon as he saw us, he flashed Grace and me a big smile.

"So *this* is your Aunt Sam," he said in a deep voice as he extended a hand toward me. "It's nice to finally meet you. I can see the family resemblance."

"Really?" I asked, taking his hand. Most people were surprised Grace and I were sisters. We both had dark blonde hair, but where she was tall and petite, I was shorter and stockier. "Most people don't."

He laughed. "It's in the smile. You three all have the same smile."

"What can we do for you, Matt?" Grace asked, leaning against the wall. I could see his cruiser sitting in a driveway a couple of houses down the street.

"I was just pulling in and saw a truck full of boxes in your driveway. I know you said your sister was coming in today, and I wondered if I could help carry some stuff in." He gave a warm smile. I felt like I had walked into some 1950's sitcom where the sheriff really was everybody's friend. I wondered if all sheriffs in small towns were like this.

"Thanks, Matt, but I don't think Sam has that much," Grace said. "She's only staying for a little while."

"Erm, well, actually..." I blushed. Grace knew I was coming to visit, but she didn't think I would actually move in. She had mentioned it, but had never officially asked. The ache in her voice when she had called to ask me for 'just a couple days' had told me she needed more than that. "It would be great to have a little help."

Grace frowned and popped her head out the door to get a look at my very full truck.

"Yeah, there is more in there than I thought. We can at least wait until it's not quite so hot out, though. How about in an hour?" Grace asked with only a hint of embarrassment.

The sheriff nodded. "I'll go change out of my work clothes and see you girls in an hour." He flashed a smile and headed back down the driveway.

"Bye, Matt!" Avery called out as he walked away.

"Is that normal?" I asked, turning to Grace.

"What?" Grace looked at me, confused.

"The sheriff just ringing your bell and asking if you need stuff unpacked? Does he help you with your groceries too?" I gave her a pointed look.

Grace rolled her eyes and shook her head. "Oh, it's not like that. He helps everybody. He and Betty were neighbors forever, and he looked out for her. When we moved in, he started keeping tabs on us too. He's more like a big brother than anything."

Grace waved her hand to dismiss whatever ideas might be brewing in my head. "Besides, he's too old for me."

"He is kind of cute," I murmured, peeking out the window to watch him walk away. He moved confidently, but with a slight limp.

"Too old. And what is all your stuff doing in the driveway, Sam?" Grace glared at me. Avery went to the window and acted like she wasn't listening.

"I came to help you. You asked if I could," I replied nonchalantly.

Grace didn't buy it for a second. "I asked if you could come and help me out *if* you had time. You are supposed to be racing this summer -- you said it was supposed to be your best season yet!" Her voice's pitch rose like our mom's used to when she was angry.

"I told you Cora got hurt. When the doctors told the sponsors she wasn't going to be racing this season, they backed out." I shrugged and walked to the kitchen, but Grace grabbed my shoulder and spun me around to face her.

"So get a new sailing partner. You are good at sailing, Sam. I won't have you waste your season just because I need a babysitter." Her blue eyes searched mine.

"I can't," I said. "The season was already in session when she got hurt, and it just isn't possible, okay? I don't want to talk about it. Just know that my racing season was already over when you called. At least here I can help you out." I shrugged like it was nothing, but it killed me inside. "Let me at least salvage something from this summer."

This was supposed to be my year. Cora and I had flown up the rankings last year, and the season had been ours for the taking. Then Cora went swimming with some friends, dove into shallow water, and injured her back. The doctors said she was lucky she was still able to breathe on her own and that she would walk again with some therapy. Her sailing days were over, and so was our partnership. I might have found someone else to sail with if the sponsors hadn't backed out, but without them, I didn't have a boat. It was one of those horrible series of events that just spiraled out of my control.

Grace glared at me. I knew she was angry that I was there. I was supposed to be sailing and going to school, not coming home to help raise a child. I knew that Grace was strong and smart enough to do it on her own, but I didn't want her to put herself through that. She had started nursing school last year so she could give Avery a better life, and I knew that if she didn't have someone to help watch Avery while she was in class, then she would have to quit. My dreams were already on hold; I didn't see a reason to postpone hers too.

"I am not happy about this, Sam, but I'll take it." Grace's eyes fell to the floor for a moment before meeting mine again. "You can have Betty's room."

Grace relaxed when I wrapped my reassuring arms around her. She needed me. And in all honesty, I needed her and Avery. With my racing season and sailing future in shambles, I needed something to keep me going. Avery was the perfect reason.

"I seem to recall someone saying there were chocolate chip cookies," I said to my older sister. "I haven't gotten one yet, and that sounds delicious."

I pretended not to notice she wiped her cheek with the back of her hand.

"They should be finished cooling. Come on, you two, we should eat them while they're still warm." Grace squeezed my shoulder and let Avery run in front of us to the kitchen. I smiled. I could get used to calling this place home.

~

The sheriff returned to our porch in exactly one hour. He wore a white t-shirt with a fishing logo, a pair of khaki shorts, and a ball cap with the same fishing logo as the shirt. Even wearing very casual clothing, he still somehow managed to exude an aura of authority. He quickly looked at my messy packing and figured out the best way to get everything into the house. Avery, Grace, and I followed his orders as he handed boxes off the truck and kept us moving. His methodical ways had the truck unpacked and in the house in almost no time.

"I just realized I didn't actually introduce myself when we first met," he said to me as he lifted the last box from the truck. Grace and Avery had gone inside to get more lemonade and cookies ready. "I'm Matt Grinswald. I'm the sheriff here in town."

"Nice to meet you, Sheriff Matt," I answered with a grin. He laughed and hoisted the box onto his shoulder. Despite the limp, he carried the heavy boxes with ease.

"Your sister says you race sailboats?"

"Yup. I like to sail double-handed races. So, two sailors on one boat." I held the front door open as he walked in. The box joined a neat pile in the room that was once Betty's. I wasn't looking forward to unpacking, but at least everything was out of the truck. It was a good thing too because rain started to splatter on the windows. We walked into the living room where Avery sprawled across the couch, tired from carrying in boxes. Grace was bustling around in the kitchen.

"You'll like our marina here then. I'm told it's perfect for sailboats. I prefer something with a motor myself, but Robbie says it's the whole reason he docks here," Sheriff Matt said.

I felt a shiver go through me. No way was he talking about *my* Robbie.

"Robbie?" I asked, trying to keep my voice level.

"Yeah, Robbie Saunders. He keeps a boat here when he's not racing. I don't give him any trouble, though. I know he's a billionaire and all famous, but around here, we treat him like he's local." Sheriff Matt gave me a serious look. "He's part of the town, and I don't like people messing with him."

"Oh, I won't bother him. I've actually met him already; I used to sail with him when we were kids." I said it like it was nothing; like Robbie hadn't been my best friend. I said it like I hadn't tried to contact him and failed. I had given up on ever finding him and talking to him. And here he was in my new little town. Fate was funny sometimes.

"Well, when he finishes his racing season, you'll have to go say hello. He usually shows up in town around mid-September. He's a good kid. Takes himself way too seriously, but he's got a good heart. He's been real good to the town. He's even donated a wing to the hospital and keeps the marina in good condition."

I nodded. Sheriff Matt continued on about the marina and the town, but I stopped listening. My brain raced. After we had moved, Robbie and I lost contact with one another. I had tried calling him a few times like when my parents died, but it had been a long time and his number had changed. I figured he had probably forgotten about me anyway. I had looked him up on the Internet, but all I ever found was his racing stats and tabloid rumors. After so many years of us being apart, it felt strange that I could run into him again. I wondered what he was up to, and if he was happy.

"Do you have a boat?" Sheriff Matt asked. I realized he had actually asked twice, but I was so lost in my own thoughts that I hadn't heard him the first time.

"No, I don't. I don't like to sail alone, so there isn't much point in me having one all to myself."

He nodded as if he understood. There was a lot more to it than that, but I didn't want to get into it. Thunder rattled the window panes, and Sheriff Matt peered out into the storm. His phone went off, buzzing in his shorts pocket.

"I figured that was going to happen. We're short-staffed today, so I'm on call if anything happens, and something always happens during a storm." He hit a button on the phone to check the message, and then put it back in his pocket with a sigh. "I'm needed at the station."

"Thank you for helping us get everything in before the storm hit," I told him with a smile. He waved his hand as though it were nothing.

"That's what neighbors are for. It was a pleasure to meet you, Sam. Avery, Grace, good to see you," he said, tipping his baseball cap. He picked up a cookie from the tray and headed to the front door. Avery waved from the couch as he stepped out into the storm.

I closed the door carefully behind him and went to my new room. Grace started working on dinner while I began to unpack the mounds of boxes. My mind still buzzed with the idea of possibly running into Robbie again. Despite the years, I missed one of the best things from my childhood: our friendship. I didn't hold out any hope he would remember his old sailing partner or the girl who gave him his first kiss. He was a billionaire and professional sailor, while I was just some girl he used to know.

Opening a suitcase and hanging the clothes in the closet, I wondered if he had ever tried calling me. We had moved all over the country when my dad started his new business, and our phone numbers kept changing. I eventually gave up learning our new addresses. I used to pretend Robbie called one of those numbers to look for me, but I knew he was probably too busy. As time went on, the possibility of the two of us ever reconnecting became slim. We had been just kids, and kids grow up. They change. They find new friends and forget the old ones; it was just the way the world worked.

"Dinner's ready," Grace called from the kitchen. I glanced around the room, already imagining my things hanging on the wall. I felt comfortable here. A soft smile crossed my face as I headed toward the dinner table. I felt comfortable here. Even if this wasn't where I wanted to be, I knew it was where I belonged.

CHAPTER 3

"Bye, Mike, I'll see you in a few hours," I called out to my boss, stepping out of the restaurant and into the warm autumn sunshine. The job at the restaurant wasn't the best, but it had paid the bills over the summer. Fall was just starting to touch the trees, turning them into glorious balls of fire against the blue sky. The change had come early this year, but I was enjoying the extra color in the trees.

"Make sure you're back in time!" Mike yelled after me. I raised my hand to acknowledge him, but I kept on walking. I had three hours before I had to pick up Avery, and then once her mom got home, I had to go back to the restaurant for a second shift. It was going to be a long day, but the extra time was going to ensure we could pay the bills this month.

I walked down the pier, heading to a small shack by the water. It was technically for boats bringing fresh fish in to the restaurant, but it was the perfect place for me to store my windsurfing gear during a shift. I had three hours, and the waves were calling my name.

"You heading out, Sam?" A strong, masculine voice asked

from behind my shoulder. I turned to see Sheriff Matt, sitting on a bench overlooking the water. I grinned and went over to talk to him.

"Yup, I've got a couple of hours before I have to pick up Avery, and I thought I would go play in the water while it's still warm. How are you doing?" I asked.

"Doing quite well. Today's my day off, so I'm here enjoying the scenery. Might even go fishing off the docks in a bit. I caught a nice big bass there the other day, and I'm hoping he had some friends." The tall man gave me a big smile and adjusted his baseball cap.

"Well, I hope you catch them. Be sure to throw the little ones back, or they'll take away your fishing license," I teased him. He laughed.

"Always do. Speaking of little ones, how's Avery doing? Is she liking school?"

"She loves it. I'm so glad we were able to get her into the accelerated program. The teachers can't stop talking about how smart she is, and she can't stop showing me all the stuff she's learning. It's adorable." I grinned at Sheriff Matt. Avery was the bright spot in my world. She had made moving to Winchester worth it.

"That's so awesome. I'm glad that's working out," he said. He paused before asking, "I know it's a sore subject, but how's the racing looking for you? Your old sailing partner doing any better?"

I sighed. "No. The doctors say that Cora might be able to sail next season, but it will depend on how she does in rehab this winter." The loss of this season stung, and the idea that I might not get to sail with Cora next year only made it worse.

Sheriff Matt nodded, his face crinkling in commiseration before shifting into a frown at something behind me.

"There goes Robbie Saunders. It's a little early in the day, but what else does a billionaire have to do?" Sheriff Matt asked. I turned to see what appeared to be a very drunk Robbie weaving his way down the dock toward his boat. He stumbled, nearly eating it on the wooden platform, but he managed to get onto his yacht and disappear below.

I had only run into him once since moving to town. He had been tying his boat to the docks when I had walked by with my windsurfing board. We had made eye contact, but neither one of us knew what to say. I hadn't talked to him since that day I left him on the dock, the bucket at his feet. I had hurried off into the water, unable to think of anything to say.

"Do you think he's going to take his boat out? I mean, he's trashed," I asked Sheriff Matt. I couldn't see the stickler-for-rules Robbie I had known doing that, but I didn't know him personally anymore. People change after ten years.

"No. He won't take it out. You're new here, but never worry about Robbie drinking and sailing. He's trouble on land. Bar fights, public intoxication-- he's always in trouble with me and the rest of the boys. But the Coast Guard loves him. He's the perfect sailor and refuses to let anyone touch the sails if they've had a sip of alcohol." The sheriff shook his head and continued, "He helps with marine rescues and even received a commendation last year. He's a model citizen on the water. There's no way he takes that boat out inebriated." Matt leaned back on the bench, crossing his arms over his burly chest.

I nodded as he spoke. I could tell from Robbie's sailing interviews online that his rule on no sailing with alcohol was something that he prided himself on. I figured he must just be settling down in his boat and sleeping it off.

"He always was a saint on the water," I murmured softly.

A ghost of a smile crossed my face as I remembered how the two of us used to sail together. He always wanted to follow the rules and never let me get away with anything on the boat. On land, he was a devil-child, but out on the water, he was a sailing angel.

"Poor guy, though. His dad is sick," Matt said, leaning forward to catch my attention. "It's all over the tabloids. Some sort of cancer. They say his older brother Jack has already taken over their oil company. Robbie's been spending most of his time either in the bar or on his boat. It seems like he's taking it rather hard."

For a split second, I thought about following Robbie to his yacht and saying hello. My feet almost took the steps, but my brain stopped them before I actually moved. I hadn't seen him in almost eleven years. He had probably forgotten about me a long time ago. The last thing he needed was some strange girl barging onto his boat and asking him if he needed a hug.

"Mr. Saunders was always really nice. I'm sorry to hear he's not doing well." My voice was soft as I stared at Robbie's yacht, my mind far away.

"You knew Daniel Saunders? Billionaire oil mogul Daniel Saunders?" Sheriff Matt stared at me like I had grown a second head. "Why didn't you ever mention that?"

"I used to sail with Robbie and so I met his dad. His dad used to come to Robbie's races and he would take Robbie and I out sailing sometimes." I shrugged. Despite being a billionaire, Mr. Saunders had been a pretty normal dad.

"Ah, gotcha." He nodded as he remembered my friendship with Robbie, then frowned as he looked at me. "You haven't talked to him yet, have you?"

I turned back to face him, a blush creeping into my cheeks. "You are just too good at figuring people out. No, I haven't talked to him. I've been busy with work and Avery. Besides, he probably doesn't even remember me. We were just kids, and it was a long time ago."

"Sure," he said as he raised his eyebrows like he didn't believe me. He was about to say more, but his phone started to ring. He started to dig around in his pockets, cursing under his breath as the ringer stopped before he could get to it.

"I'm going to go windsurfing before I have to get back to work," I said, trying to edge away while he was busy.

"Have fun. Isn't it a little cold for surfing?" He asked, his eyes focusing on the tiny phone screen when he finally found it in his coat pocket.

"Anything to get out on the water." I grinned.

"Why don't you just go in a boat, like normal people?" he asked, pressing buttons on his phone.

"I only sail double-handed. I don't like sailing by myself," I chided him gently.

"Right, and you don't consider windsurfing to be sailing. I remember now." He smiled and replaced his phone back in the original pocket. I wondered if he would lose it again.

"It was great to see you, Sam," he said with a warm smile. "Have fun out there."

"Always do!" I flashed him a bright grin and waved as I turned and headed toward the shack storing my equipment. The ocean was calling my name and I was ready to get out on the water.

CHAPTER 4

he water slipped silently under my board as I glided out toward the open ocean. A slight breeze tugged gently at the waves, promising a fun afternoon. I couldn't wait to really let loose and speed across the water, but I wanted to get out where I could practice some of my more flamboyant moves without looking like a complete idiot in front of the entire marina.

Seeing Robbie brought back old memories, and I paddled through them as I worked my way out to where I could play in the wind.

"We are going to get through this together, Sam." My older sister's voice echoed through my mind as I was transported back in time.

> *It was three years after leaving Robbie and I had just had my fifteenth birthday. My sailing lesson was done for the day and I was out on the water by myself. I didn't want to go back in yet, so I sailed further out. There was a storm brewing, but*

it made the waves more challenging. I thought I could handle it.

The storm caught me by surprise. I had managed to pull the mainsail before the boat flipped, but the mast was broken. The ropes were now wet and slippery. I couldn't handle it on my own. I wasn't ready for a challenge like this. I wished I had someone to help me.

The waves tossed my little boat like a toy. This storm was past what I could handle. I clung to the rigging, praying that my tiny boat wouldn't capsize. I had radioed for help, but I wasn't sure anyone had heard me. Saltwater and tears burned in my eyes. I was going to drown because I had been stupid and gone out too far on my own.

A horn sounded, heavy in the storm. Relief flooded through me as a beautiful white and red Coast Guard ship shined a light on my boat. I could hear sailors yelling as they threw me a line. I was saved.

I tipped the sails on my windsurfing board into the light breeze, making me go faster as I stayed in my memories.

The Valiant brought me home, cutting through the storm as though it were nothing. The sailors deposited me, blanket-wrapped and terrified, at the dock with stern warnings to never to do that again. It was raining at the dock, but the wind was gone. A parked police cruiser was waiting to take me home, only something was wrong. Grace was in the car, her eyes red and her cheeks

splotchy. She took me into her arms, holding me close as she told me the news.

When I didn't come home after my lesson, and the reports of the storm came in, my parents had gotten in the car to come look for me. There was a horrible accident. They were gone.

I didn't believe her at first. I pushed her away and ran out into the rain. A police officer chased after me. I tripped and fell into a puddle; I didn't bother to get up. This wasn't how the day was supposed to have gone. I should have just gone home; I should never have gone into the storm. If only someone had been there to help me get the sails down, I would have made it back before they went out to look for me; if only I hadn't gone out into the storm...

The wind sent a spray of water into my face. I returned my focus to the present, letting my memories and the hurt wash away in the ocean. From the corner of my eye, I could see a boat approaching, its sails full out as it glided along. It almost looked like the yacht that I had seen Robbie enter, but I knew it couldn't be Robbie. Robbie wouldn't be sailing drunk.

My board caught a wave, stealing my attention away from the oncoming vessel. I had the right of way, so I focused on my own board instead of the boat, trying to keep from tipping over in the strong breeze. I concentrated on getting control of my sail and moving out of the way, knowing that the approaching ship could easily avoid me. The wind whistled in my ears, the ocean slapping at the board.

I turned, thinking I was clear, but the boat had moved

more quickly than I anticipated. The keel of the boat seemed bigger than I thought possible as it hurtled straight for me. Time slowed, and the details burned into my eyes: the white tips on the gray-green water, the yellow in my sail, the tiny barnacle trying to find a foothold on the keel of the oncoming yacht. There was no way to stop the collision now, and I let go of my sail, hearing it splash into the water. Robbie's eyes met mine, full of terror and recognition as his boat crashed into me, and everything went dark.

CHAPTER 5

quiet beeping and a steady hiss woke me. The late afternoon sun was shining in through the windows, coating the strange room with a buttery warmth. I blinked hard, trying to clear my vision and make sense of where I was. My nose itched, and as I rubbed at it, my fingers caught the small plastic tubing.

I frowned as I realized I was in the hospital. A large white-board on the adjacent wall proclaimed that my nurse was Jaime and my doctor was Dr. Robins. It took a moment, but I could remember his concerned face above me. He had nice eyes. I groaned and leaned back on the pillow, letting the memories of the ER wash over me. I recalled the kind brown eyes, the calls to the nursing staff and the glorious relief when they pushed some sort of liquid into the IV in my arm. The entire experience was blurry and surreal, but at least I remembered something. Grace would laugh when I told her about this.

Grace. Avery.

I sat up in a panic, adrenaline flooding through my system. I was supposed to pick Avery up from school! I glanced down at my wrist to check what time it was, but my watch was missing. The yellow late afternoon sunshine told me I was already late. Avery was probably standing on the front step of her school, little lunch box in hand, waiting for me to come get her with tears in her eyes. Grace was going to kill me.

I ripped the oxygen tubing out of my nose and threw my legs over the side of the bed. A woozy rush went through me, and my hands tightened on the sheets. I really hoped the nurses' station was close by because I wasn't going to make it far. But I had to get to Avery.

"Shh, lie back down," a soft voice said from the corner. I glanced over to see Grace starting to rise from her chair. She pushed away a hospital tray full of books and a laptop and walked over to the bed. "Avery's fine."

Grace carefully picked up my feet and deftly maneuvered me back into bed. She wrapped the oxygen neatly around my ears and under my chin, her hands sure and steady. She was going to make a great nurse one of these days.

"But I was supposed to pick her up! Grace, I'm so sorry! I..."

"Shhh. Don't worry, little sis. They called me as soon as you were out of the water. I picked her up from school on my way here." She smiled and soothed my ponytail down across my shoulder. "One of the nurses is showing her where the vending machines are. She'll be up here in a little bit."

The oxygen tickled my nose, so I tugged at it. Grace frowned and replaced it in my nose, giving me a look that told me to keep it there.

"What time is it?" I asked. "And where's my watch?"

Grace sat down on the edge of the bed. "I have your stuff

in a bag in the closet. And it's a little after three in the afternoon. Don't worry, I called your boss and told them you weren't going to make your second shift." She paused and scrunched her nose. "Your boss is kind of a jerk, by the way."

I gave a wry laugh and finally relaxed a little. "No kidding. I'll be lucky if I still have a job after this. I got run over by a boat, but since I'm missing the shift, it'll all be my fault."

"Don't worry about it. That was a temporary job anyway. I'll be done with school in a few months, and then we won't have to worry quite so much," Grace said. She patted my leg gently.

I groaned. "You had a test today, didn't you?"

She shrugged as though missing a test was nothing. "Family comes first; you know that. Besides, the professor said I could make it up. At least it was the teacher that actually likes me. If it was Mrs. Burnside, I might have had to kill you."

She said it with a straight face, but as soon as she finished she flashed me a grin. Grace was so close to finishing nursing school that she could taste it. She had doubled up on as many classes as the program would let her to finish as quickly as possible, but even so, we were struggling to make ends meet. With her school schedule, she didn't have any time to work. It was my measly waitressing job that was keeping a roof over our heads and food on our table. Once she graduated and could work as an RN, life would be much easier.

Except now, I was going to have to add whatever medical bills came out of this little trip. I pushed the thought away. The last thing I needed to be worrying about was how I was going to pay for this. My job didn't exactly offer health insurance.

"The doctor let me look at your x-rays," Grace said. She grinned excitedly, her medical streak showing through. Her little sister was in the hospital, but she was excited that she got to see the x-rays. I couldn't help but smile at her. Such a medical nerd. "You are lucky, little sis. Just a concussion, a bruised rib, a strained wrist, and a bajillion little cuts and bruises. You are going to be black and blue for a while."

"*Just* a concussion, a broken rib and a sprained wrist? Ugh, it feels like I got run over by a truck." I massaged the bandage around my wrist, noticing it for the first time. I also was noticing that breathing was actually rather uncomfortable.

"Well, you did. A boat, but same difference," Grace said with a shrug. I swatted at her and missed.

"Who hit me?" I gave a silent prayer that it wasn't Robbie. That it was just someone who looked kind of like Robbie. And drove a similar boat.

"Robbie Saunders." Grace's petite features twisted in anger. "He was drunk."

"No... He wouldn't..." I shook my head.

"Well, he did. Blew a point two," Grace said. She closed her eyes and shook her head in amazement. "He managed to pull you onto his boat and get in to shore, thank heaven. You were out cold."

"He wouldn't sail drunk..."

Grace continued as though she hadn't heard me. "Only damaged two boats pulling into the dock. Would have been three if Sheriff Grinswald hadn't been there. He put him straight in jail. It will depend on if you press charges as to whether or not he stays there." She gave me a look that said I should press the charges.

"Robbie Saunders wouldn't sail drunk," I said firmly. Grace took my bandaged hand in hers.

"He did. And he nearly got you killed because of it. I know he was your friend when you were kids, but he's different now. I'm sorry, Sam." Grace looked at me, her pale blue eyes serious. My shoulders fell. I knew it was true, but I still couldn't believe it.

The door to the room opened and a small form stood in the doorway for a moment before yelling, "AUNT SAM!" and running across the small room. She jumped up on the bed and gave me the biggest hug her small arms could manage. I hugged her back as tightly as my poor broken body would allow.

The tiny blonde-haired child let go of me and regarded me solemnly, her big blue eyes taking in all my cuts and bruises. "Mommy said you got hurt and were sleeping. I'm glad you're not dead."

Grace let out a strangled noise as she tried to keep her face straight. I grinned at my niece.

"I'm glad I'm not dead, too. I'm sorry I didn't pick you up from school and get ice cream like I promised," I told her, pulling her into a more comfortable position on my lap.

"Ice cream?" Grace asked, raising her eyebrow at me. I winced.

"Yeah... it was supposed to be our special treat today." I gave Avery's mom an apologetic smile.

"It's okay," Avery piped up. "They have lots of ice cream here! I've had three already!"

Grace's mouth opened to tell her daughter something about ruining her dinner, but at that moment the doctor walked in. He was the man I remembered from the ER, with kind brown eyes and a cheerful smile.

"Glad to see you up," Dr. Robins said as he pulled up a chair next to my bed. He pulled out a penlight, and shined it into my eyes, gauging my response. Whatever my eyes did seemed to please him, and he leaned back and smiled.

"Am I going to live, Doc?" I asked. He laughed.

"Yes, I think so," he replied. "I'm going to need you to stay overnight for observation, though. The concussion is serious enough that we want to make sure that everything is fine before we release you. Sometimes it takes a few hours for problems to appear, and we don't want any surprises."

"But, Dr. Robins, I can't..." I started.

"I'm sorry, Samantha, but this isn't negotiable. You really do need to stay here." He stood up from the chair so he could look down at me. I suddenly felt like I was a child. "You are very lucky to be alive. With the concussion and your injuries, you came very close to drowning. I don't want to scare you, but I need you to stay the night and make sure that everything is fine. If everything looks good, you can leave first thing in the morning, all right?"

I nodded meekly. There was no way I was going to be able to afford another night. *But what the heck?* I thought to myself. *There was no way I'm going to be able to afford the care I've received up to this minute; what was another few hours going to add to an already un-payable bill?* The thought didn't give me much comfort.

"Good." Dr. Robins gave a crisp nod. "I'll come check on you in the morning. Until then, I'd like you to get some rest. I'm sure Grace here has already filled you in on all your injuries, but do you have any questions for me?"

"Nope. Even if I did, I'm sure Grace will take care of me," I answered. He laughed.

"She is going to be a great nurse. You graduate in December, right?" he asked, turning toward Grace. She blushed and nodded.

"My mommy said I can keep her nursing hat when she graduates!" Avery chirped from my lap.

"I'm sure you will both look fantastic in it. If you need a recommendation for the scholarship, I'd be more than happy to write one for you. It's been a pleasure having you do your nursing rotations here," Dr. Robins said, a smile on his face. Grace laughed nervously.

"I will be sure to do that. Thank you again, Doctor," she said. I could see her blush creeping further up her throat.

"My pleasure. I'll come check on you in the morning, Samantha." Dr. Robins gave us all a big smile and turned and walked out the door, humming softly as he closed it behind him.

"A scholarship recommendation?" I asked Grace, raising my eyebrows at her. Avery giggled.

"Mommy thinks he's cute," Avery whispered.

"Hey!" Grace's voice came out a squeak, which made Avery giggle again.

"Oh, so 'scholarship recommendation' is the new code word for secret crush," I said, turning to Avery.

"Quit it, you two!" Grace shouted, her face turning an even more delightful shade of red. "He just works on this floor and he is very nice. You two stop making insinuations!"

"What's an in-sin-u-a-tion?" Avery whispered, sounding out the word carefully.

"It's when you say one thing, but really mean another," I whispered back. She nodded.

"So what is this scholarship? You graduate at the end of the semester-- why would you need a scholarship?" I asked, wrapping my arms around Avery. The little girl leaned back into me, watching her mom.

"It's a repayment scholarship. Kind of like a paid internship," Grace answered. "Three students of the nursing program get full tuition reimbursement and a job here at the hospital. It also puts them on the fast track for a nursing management position."

"So it's a really-awesome-program-that-is-right-up-your-alley-and-having-cutie-doctor-give-you-a-recommendation kind of thing?" I teased. Grace rolled her eyes at me.

"Yes. It's just that it's super competitive, and even with 'cutie doctor's' recommendation, I probably won't get it," she said.

"So, you're not even going to try? Come on, Grace!" I gave her a stern look. "The cute doctor thinks you have a shot. At least have him write you a nice letter. If nothing else, you might get a date out of it. At best, you might actually get the dang thing."

"But, Sam..."

"No 'buts'! How come I am just hearing about this?"

"Like I said, it's a really prestigious thing... I'm not the top in my class, and while I have some recommendations, I'm not the pick of the litter. I didn't tell you because I knew you'd push me to do it and I didn't want to get your hopes up." Grace paused and looked down at her hands. "You've been working so hard to keep us afloat, and I didn't want to let you down."

"I think you could do it, Mommy," Avery said quietly. The corners of Grace's mouth twitched upward at her daughter's comment.

"Me too. Go get that doctor's number. Or something," I told her.

Grace rolled her eyes at me and held out her hands to Avery. "We gotta get going, little girl. Your aunt needs some rest," she said.

"And we gotta catch a doctor," Avery responded. I gave her a hug before she jumped off my lap.

"That's my girl," I said as she landed on the floor and took her mother's hand.

"You two are awful," Grace said. I could practically hear her eyes roll in her head. "Don't you worry about the money right now, little sis. We'll make it work somehow. We always do. You just rest and we'll figure things out later."

I nodded.

"Bye, Aunt Sam! I'll see you tomorrow. Maybe we can go get ice cream then!" Avery called as they walked out the door.

I tried to settle down, but even so it was hard. Grace was right, though. There was no point in worrying at the moment since there wasn't anything I could do about it. But that didn't stop the trickle of panic from worming its way into my brain.

~

I stared at the book the nurse had given me, but I wasn't really reading the page. It was some sort of romance novel, but I wasn't looking for love. I was looking for something to keep myself from freaking out. Despite Grace's calm assertion that we would somehow make it work, I was panicking. My boss was pissed, if the two voice-mails and three texts complaining about my not being there were any indication. He was probably going to fire me. Or at least reduce my hours for being "unreliable." I wanted to scream.

My extra shift was supposed to make sure that rent and Avery's private school tuition were going to get paid without us having to skimp on groceries. It was going to be another lean month, especially since I knew my boss wouldn't schedule me for an extra shift ever again. Throw in the lack of health insurance, and this medical bill-- I was going to be broke until I was a hundred and two.

A knock on the door caught my attention and made me look up. An attractive woman in her late forties entered the room, a shy smile playing across her face. Her dark hair was pulled up neatly into a bun, and stylish square glasses accented her big, brown eyes. She looked familiar; something about her smile and the confident way she carried herself.

"Hi, Samantha. I don't know if you remember me, but I would like to talk to you about Robbie," the woman said confidently. It was the voice coupled with the designer suit that made me remember her.

"You're Rachel. Of course I remember you. You would always let Robbie and me stop at the ice cream shop on our way home after sailing lessons. And you are one of the few people that always insisted on calling me Samantha instead of just Sam." I gave her a warm grin and sat up taller in the bed. Rachel sat down carefully in the chair that Grace had vacated only an hour before.

"I'm glad you remember me. I need to talk to you about Robbie, and I'll need you to sign some paperwork," she said, pulling a folder out of an oversized purse.

"I still can't believe he hit me. I mean, they told me he was drinking, but..." I shook my head slowly. "What happened to him, Rachel? I mean, why would he do that? It's just not like him."

Rachel sat very still for a moment, her brow furrowing slightly as she appraised me. I had always liked her when Robbie and I were kids. Rachel was one of the few people that Robbie always listened to, and as such, he always behaved for her. She had a fantastic sense of humor and could always send the two of us into hysterics.

"His dad is dying. He's having a hard time dealing with it. That's not an excuse or a justification, just the explanation," she added quickly. She pointed to the file now sitting on my hospital table. "I'd like to ask you not to press charges. The Saunders' family would like to reimburse you for all medical expenses, including any future care you may need with regard to this injury, as well as a payment to cover any work-related expenses this injury may have incurred."

Reimburse you for all medical expenses and *payment to cover any work related expenses* were the only words I heard. This could fix everything if I played my cards right.

"And if I said I still wanted to press charges, would I get all the shiny prizes?"

Rachel's eyebrows raised, and she cocked her head. "Yes. The Saunders family feels that they should make sure this accident does not end up changing your life. If you still feel the need to press charges and change Robbie's life, then that is purely your decision."

Her answer was obviously rehearsed, but it was what I wanted to hear. This wasn't supposed to be a bribe, but it was exactly what Grace, Avery, and I needed.

"I never intended to press charges against him. Call me sentimental, but I still consider him a friend." I shrugged. "I know that he must be going through something crazy hard if he broke his own rule. Besides, he saved me from drowning, so I would like to be able to thank him for that, even if he was the one who put me in the water."

Rachel's shoulders instantly relaxed. "Thank you. I really mean it too, not just as the Saunders' family representative, but as Robbie's friend. Thank you."

I remembered the skinny little boy with the bucket rolling around his feet. He was my best friend then, and I hadn't had another like him since. "He's my friend. Or at least he was a long time ago. And friends help each other with mistakes. He got me out of trouble a couple of times too."

Rachel looked for a moment as though she might ask what kind of trouble we had gotten into, but then she thought better of it. I grinned. There were things that would still get the two of us in trouble today if she found out about them.

"Out of curiosity, how much *is* the payment?" I asked.

Rachel answered, saying the number as though it were nothing. "Our standard is twenty-five thousand dollars. If you don't think that is going to be enough, I can always speak with the Saunders' lawyer and come up with a more equitable figure."

I swallowed hard. That was my year's salary. That would keep the roof over our head and groceries on the table. That would even get Avery a pretty decent Christmas. I tried to keep the excitement out of my voice. "Twenty-five thousand dollars? No, that's fine. That amount is just fine. It's good."

The rest of the meeting with Rachel went by in a blur. I read the papers as she put them in front of me; I didn't want to sign away my first-born or agree to donate a kidney if it was in the fine print. She waited patiently, indicating where I should sign and then collecting the forms in a neat stack.

"Thank you, Samantha. Can I get you anything before I go?" she asked.

"No thanks," I said, but then I thought of Robbie. If he was still the same caring person I knew as a kid, this would be eating him up from the inside. "Are you going to go see Robbie?"

She nodded, stowing her stylish glasses into a designer case and slipping them into the giant bag she called a purse.

"When you see him, will you tell him I'm all right? And

that I'm not angry. I'd really like it if he came and visited me. For old time's sake." I hoped that wasn't overstepping some boundary, but despite everything that had happened, I wanted to see my old friend.

Rachel gave me a warm smile. "You got it. I'm sure he'll want to see you." She shouldered her bag and stood to leave. "Thank you again, Samantha. I hope I get to see you again soon, though preferably not in the hospital next time."

I laughed as she left the room, carefully closing the door behind her. I stared at the wooden door, a sense of relief flooding through me. *Twenty-five. Thousand. Dollars!* With that much money, I could relax. The medical bills weren't going to be a problem. While getting in a boat accident wasn't my idea of a lucky break, things were starting to look up.

CHAPTER 6

The water splashes against the hull of my boat, a soft comforting sound. The sky is bright blue without a cloud in sight. I am at peace. This part of the dream is always pleasant. I like this part of the dream. Evan is alive and happy with Grace. Mom and Dad are safe at home, and we are going to have meatloaf for dinner.

Then, the rigging starts to tangle. Impossible knots form on the lines, turning the sails into flying monsters that catch the wind and threaten to tear my boat apart. A storm is rising from the depths of hell, the sky going black in an instant. The peace and calm is gone. I have to move quickly; if I'm fast enough, I can escape the storm before it gets to me. If I just go fast enough, maybe this time I can avoid the storm. My hands fumble on the rigging, and every movement seems delayed.

Wind howls through the now ripped and tangled sails, and giant waves slosh over the deck, threatening my every step. I wasn't fast enough. The storm has found me, and I can't escape it. If I had help, I would have made it, but by myself, I am too slow. I cling desperately to the mast, praying that the storm will stop.

I see my parents, sailing on a boat in the distance. Dad is at the helm, tied to the wheel as he tries to steer into the storm. I scream at him, but he doesn't hear. Mom turns and waves, the wind and rain twisting her hair, but she smiles at me. She taps Dad on the shoulder, then points toward me. Her sundress flaps in the hurricane winds, but she looks toward my boat with relief. They were looking for me.

Dad turns the boat and smiles, his eyes twinkling as he carefully makes his way across the choppy water. He doesn't see the ropes holding him down. They don't seem concerned with the storm raging around them. Lightning flashes and a gaping hole appears in their hull, water surging inside their small vessel. They are going to drown.

I scream, wrenching my yellow sails to reach them faster, praying myself ragged that they'll let me get to them in time. Dad turns his head, confusion crossing his face as the water laps at his ankles. He keeps going, my mother urging him toward me. They are so close, but in this storm, they are never going to make it. Their ship sinks lower and lower, the dark waves gobbling it up long before I can reach it. They're gone, the water devours them as though they never existed.

I sob, holding onto the main mast as my boat creaks and groans beneath me, barely staying afloat in the raging sea. They are gone and I am alone. But then, a beam of light cuts through the darkness. A new boat is coming, someone who can save me. Hope bubbles up within me and I stand tall. Evan stands on the prow of a mighty ship, his hand shielding his eyes from the spray. His Army dress uniform is beautiful and perfect, the way it was at his funeral. He points toward me, and his ship turns. I'm saved.

Lightning flashes, a hot thin jagged line of molten light crashing into Evan's ship. He looks back at it, his face contorting with terror. His ship is on fire. Orange and red flames engulf his ship in fire and he screams, sinking quickly into the black raging *waters. I can see the light of the fire slowly fade into the black depths swallowed it completely.*

I'm alone again. I have no sails left. The wind keeps on howling, and the rain stings as it hits me. I know that if someone else were here, this never would have happened. It's all my fault that I couldn't reach them in time. I wasn't fast enough to save them. I know in my bones that if someone had been there to help me trim the sails, I never would have hit that storm. I would have gotten home before anyone would have gone out to look for me. My parents never would have been out in that storm if it weren't for me. If they had survived, Evan wouldn't have joined the Army. He'd still be here too.

It was all my fault because I had sailed alone.

CHAPTER 7

woke up in a cold sweat. The hospital room was unfamiliar at first, but moonlight from the window illuminated the room. I heard a quiet beeping at the nurses' station, and soft voices down the hall. I was safe. There was no storm. I willed my heartbeat to slow before it pounded out of my chest, but I knew I would have a hard time falling back asleep. I always did.

I hated that nightmare. It had started the day after my parents died. Grace insisted it wasn't my fault, but only a part of me believed her. My parents had gone out in the storm to look for me. I was the reason they were on the road the night their car crashed. If I hadn't been sailing by myself, if I hadn't been stupid enough to get caught in the storm, then they would never have been out in the rain. Their brakes would never have failed and that tree would have fallen on empty road. If someone had been out on that boat with me, they wouldn't have been so worried. I might not have even been in the storm in the first place.

No, despite Grace's kind words, their death was my fault. I sailed into a storm by myself, and they were worried. If someone had been with me, then everything would be different. The day they died, I swore never to sail alone.

The nightmare had stopped while Evan was with us. The first three years of Avery's life, the nightmares were gone. Evan kept us safe. I always sailed with someone, and things were going well. But then Evan died. I came home from a rough race to Grace's tear stained face and a man in a crisp uniform. My nightmare came back that night, and Evan became a part of it.

I flipped my pillow over, searching for the cool side. It always took me a while to fall back asleep after the nightmare. I hadn't had it for a few months, but with the recent accident, I could see why my brain had dredged it up. The sails being yellow, like my windsurfing sails, was the obvious connection between the nightmares and my accident.

I closed my eyes and tried to focus on my breathing.

My eyes were growing heavy as I concentrated on keeping my breathing even. I had to be calm going back to sleep, or I'd fall into the nightmare again. It was a risk I took while trying to find rest again. Once the nightmare debuted for the night, it often stayed and replayed itself until morning. I was just drowsing off when a nurse popped her head into my room. She walked over and gently put her hand on my shoulder.

"I'm sorry, sweetie, but we have to do another concussion check," she whispered. I groaned and opened my eyes. At this rate, I was never going to get any sleep.

The nurse turned on the bathroom light, the weak yellow bulb casting strange shadows across the room. I sat up, getting ready to answer her questions and let her check my pupils; I yawned, but was actually okay with the fact she was keeping me up. If I was awake, I couldn't get stuck in the storm of my nightmare.

CHAPTER 8

I lay in bed watching bad TV. Some girl was waiting to hear the paternity test results for her baby and had narrowed it down to five possible guys. I shook my head at her, wondering exactly how she got herself into that situation. Two guys, I could understand. But five? That must have been some party. At least a celebrity dancing show was supposed to be on next. That I could understand.

I glanced at the clock. It was still early afternoon, but I was ready to get home. The concussion checks, as well as my nightmares, had made for a poor night's sleep, and the food was the usual terrible hospital fare. I was looking forward to going home to my own bed and my own fridge. As soon as the doctor came by to release me, I could leave. It was going to be a little while, though, as the nurses said he was stuck on an emergency case. Since the Saunders were covering my medical bills, I didn't really mind the wait. If nothing else, I was catching up on my trashy TV.

A soft knock on my door drew my attention. I was all dressed and ready to go, in just comfortable jeans and a t-shirt, but I still smoothed the front of my shirt. Hopefully it was the doctor coming to release me. I didn't want to have hospital food for dinner if I didn't have to.

"Come in," I called. The door opened slowly, and a tall figure stood in the doorway for a moment before stepping inside. It was Robbie. He closed the door carefully behind him, coming into the main area of the room and standing there awkwardly. I fumbled with the TV remote, finding the mute button first.

Robbie stood at the foot of my bed. The collar was crooked on his polo shirt, and wrinkles lined his pants; it looked as though he had slept in his clothes from the night before. I wondered when the last time he had shaved had been, as his five-o'clock shadow was more like a five-day shadow. It matched his sandy hair, messed and unruly. He didn't make eye contact, instead looking at the foot of my bed, his whole body radiating sorrow and regret.

"I'm not really sure why I'm here, but... I didn't know where else to go. I'll leave if you don't want me here." His voice was low and full of restrained heartache. It sounded as if he had been crying, and given that his eyes were red and his hair disheveled, I certainly thought he had been. I wanted to stand up and give him a hug, to comfort the misery hanging heavy on his shoulders, but I made myself stay in bed. Just because I still thought of him as a friend, it didn't negate the fact we hadn't spoken in years.

"No, don't go. Here, have a seat," I offered, pointing to one of the chairs next to my bed. He stared at it for a moment before moving slowly. He sat gingerly, as though I might change my mind at any second and ask him to leave. We sat in silence for a moment.

"The doctor said I should have drowned out there, and Grace told me you pulled me from the water. Did you really save me?" I asked him. I was still trying to make sense of the whole event. I remembered the pull of the water, and strong arms around me holding me up to the air. There was pain and the water was so cold. It was difficult to put the pieces of my fuzzy memory back into place and I was still trying to understand how it all happened.

Robbie frowned, staring at his feet. "If you mean, crashed into you, knocked you unconscious and then had the decency to dive in and get you out of the mess I created, then yes. I saved you. But I'm not a hero. Not by a long shot."

"Well, thank you for not letting me drown. I appreciate that," I said, a smile playing on my face. I reached out and put a hand on his shoulder, but he just kept staring at the floor.

"I want to apologize to you. I know Rachel came down, and that you reached an agreement with her, but I wanted to apologize in person. This never should have happened, and I can't begin to tell you how incredibly sorry I am." He looked up at me, his green eyes bright with regret. "You are the last person I would ever want to hurt."

A smile curved on my lips. Those green eyes were the same ones I remembered. There was a boyish spark in them, and I didn't want to look away. I knew I should be angry with him, that I had every right to be furious, but I wasn't. I had tried all night to be mad at him, but instead, I had found myself worrying about him.

"You know I could never stay mad at you," I said softly. I gave his shoulder a slight squeeze. "Rachel said your dad is sick. I can understand the pain that causes. Pain makes you do crazy, stupid things."

He nodded, looking down again. "Yeah... I thought he hated me and he was just getting sicker. The idea that he was going to leave thinking I was a failure... I just wanted to go out on the water where I could think."

A tear slid down his face, dripping onto the floor. He wiped it off with the back of his hand and crossed his arms to his chest. I looked away and glanced up at the TV, giving him a moment to recover. A man was speaking into the camera, but the caption underneath told me why Robbie was so upset: "Breaking News: Billionaire Oil Mogul Daniel Saunders Dead at Age 67."

"Oh, Robbie, I'm so sorry," I whispered as I turned back to him, his eyes up on the TV.

"His last words to me were that he was proud of me. That I didn't disappoint him. He said he loved me." Robbie's voice cracked with emotion. I moved my hand to his, and he held it as though I were his lifeline. His eyes were also up on the television screen, glued to the picture of his father, as he let the words inside of him spill out. I stayed quiet, letting him give voice to the pain.

"I thought he hated me for so long. My whole life, everything was always about Jack and the company. I hated that stupid oil company. It always felt like he loved it more than me. That he had more time for his company than he did for his own son." Robbie paused for a moment and I hit the power button on the remote. The screen faded to black, but he kept staring up at it.

"Last night, I went to see him. We talked for hours, and he actually listened. We talked about sailing and racing, and... he was the father I remembered having as a little kid. He was the one who got me into sailing in the first place. We used to go out, just the two of us, on his boat and just see how fast we could sail around the bay. Jack hated getting up that early, and Mom never liked to sail, so it was just us." Robbie's eyes clouded as he sailed in his memory.

I gave his hand a light squeeze but didn't say anything. He just needed me to listen and be there for him. I had no words to tell him anyway, no way to take the sting from this passing. He just needed someone to understand and let him talk.

"I don't know when we stopped doing that. We just didn't go anymore, and then things went downhill from there. He got so busy with Jack, and I was forgotten. Nothing I did was ever good enough, and if it didn't have to do with the company, no one was interested. I was so sure he hated me. But he didn't." Robbie paused, and looked over at me. "I don't know why I'm telling you this. Or even why I'm here. It just felt right to come and tell you, though. Maybe it's just to explain what I've done."

"It's okay. You can tell me anything. It's been a while, but I'm still your first mate," I said. His hand tightened around mine, his skin growing warmer the longer we touched.

We sat there, our fingers wrapped around one another as the sun slanted through the window, the world awash in orange fire. He might be taller and stronger now, but this was still my Robbie. It was as if no time had passed while we were apart; the two of us came back together as easily as if it had been days instead of years. The connection that we shared was still there, and we didn't even have to talk to find it.

We would have sat there like that into the night, except the nurse came by to tell me the doctor was finally on his way. Robbie roused himself as though he had been lost to a deep sleep and stood once the nurse left. I felt a small twinge of sadness as he let go of my hand.

"Thank you," he said. He managed a sad smile, and ran his fingers through his short, sandy colored hair.

"Anytime. It was actually really nice to see you." My

fingers started playing with the end of my ponytail, and I bit my lip. I really wanted to see him again.

"Would it be okay if I saw you again?" he asked, as though he had heard the words inside my mind. I couldn't have stopped the smile that spread across my face even if I had wanted to.

"I would like that very much. I've missed you, Robbie."

"I've missed you too, Sam. I tried to find you after you moved, but my calls never went through." His legs pressed against the bed as he looked down at me. A surge of happiness went through me that he had looked for me too. "Things are always better when you're around."

He paused, as though he wanted to say more, but then Dr. Robins walked into the room. Robbie nodded to doctor and raised his hand in a wave as he headed toward the door. "I'll see you soon, Sam," he called. And then he was gone again.

Dr. Robins began asking me questions, checking me out one last time so I could go home, but my mind wasn't on him. It was on the man that I knew as the boy with the bucket at his feet.

CHAPTER 9

I blinked as I stepped into the bright afternoon. After the dim restaurant, the sunlight seemed almost unnaturally bright. The sky was still a cloudless blue, and the water smelled salty and clean as it came off the ocean. The afternoon was almost unseasonably warm, and it felt surreal to have the warmth with the fall colors filling the trees. Despite my manager's best efforts to make my life miserable, it was a beautiful day.

"And Sam, if you miss another shift-- you're fired!" Mike called out before the door swung shut. I didn't even turn around; I just kept walking. It was a gorgeous day, and I wasn't about to let him spoil it. He had been pissed about my missed shifts and had cut my hours just like I suspected he would. Normally, I would have been panicking, but I knew the money Rachel had promised had already been wired into my bank account.

The freedom of knowing that my credit cards were going to be paid off and that the tuition for Avery's private school was covered, despite losing my work hours, was fantastic. I could hop, skip, and sing because I knew I had at least a little bit of financial flexibility.

I hummed softly as I walked along the dock. Fishing boats bobbed gently in the distance, the white of their paint like extra wave caps in the distance. It was a perfect afternoon. If I had my windsurfing gear, I would have been out on the water in an instant.

I stumbled on a loose board, catching myself before I fell. My side burned and I grimaced, pressing my hand into my bruised rib. The rib was healing, but it still hurt if I breathed in too deeply. My wrist was no longer swollen, but I was still babying it. A couple of days more, and the bruises would be faded and I'd be back to my old self. In a week, no one would even be able to tell I had been in an accident in the first place.

I waved to Sheriff Matt as I walked up alongside his boat. It was a simple motor boat, perfect for fishing and day trips. I could see his poles and gear all stashed neatly in a corner as he pulled into his slip.

"Catch anything good?" I called out, grabbing his line as he threw it toward shore. I deftly secured his small fishing boat as he hopped onto the dock, carrying a cooler of fish.

"A couple of bass. You want one? I end up storing half of what I catch in my freezer until I'm sick to death of fish. You and your sister can have one on me," he offered. I thought about it for a moment but shook my head.

"Avery is going through a phase where, in addition to only wearing her princess costume, she will only eat things that are orange or green. Or chocolate." I gave him a smile. "So unless your bass is orange, green or made of chocolate, I'm afraid it won't get eaten at our house. Thank you, though."

Sheriff Matt laughed. "No problem. I'm sure I'll find

something to do with it." He looked me over, obviously checking to make sure I wasn't still banged up from the accident. "How's Robbie doing? I haven't seen him for a couple of days, but I heard he stopped by the hospital to see you."

"He did. He's having a hard time getting over his dad's death. I think it's gonna take him a while to really accept it. At least they went out on good terms, but... I know how hard it can be to lose a parent. It hurts so deep, and that just never goes away." I looked down at the wooden planks, remembering my own grief. My heart ached for Robbie. This wasn't something that could simply be gotten over. "I'm supposed to meet up with him later this week. I'll tell him you said hi."

"I'm sure he'll just love that," Sheriff Matt said, rolling his eyes. "He's got potential. I just wish he'd see that. You sure you don't want a fish?"

"Yes, I'm sure," I said, nodding vigorously.

"I'll see you around, then. Have a good afternoon," the sheriff called out as he limped back toward the County Jail. I watched him for a moment. I knew he had been in the Army, but he never spoke about his injury. The way his eyes clouded whenever anyone mentioned it, though, I had a feeling it was not just a physical injury that caused the pain.

I continued along the dock. The smell of fish and seaweed brought back happy memories of my childhood. I had spent most of my days out on the ocean, playing with Robbie on boats or in the water. Even at school, sailing was all that Robbie and I ever talked about. We had big plans to sail across the ocean and see the world. Those plans had seemed so important back then.

I came around to a marina slip that was usually empty. I considered it my "dream" stall. It was where I liked to launch my windsurfing gear, and where I someday hoped to put a boat of my own. Where I was expecting an empty space, a beautiful, shiny new J111 racing sailboat sat bobbing gently.

I whistled softly, looking her up and down. She was just big enough that you could fit a party on the deck, but small enough that two could easily sail her. She had a strong, tall mast and what looked like new sails. I knew from experience that when properly handled, she would fly like the wind across the water. She was a beautiful, fast racing boat.

"Do you like it?" Robbie asked, stepping out from behind me. He had on his typical sailing gear of windbreaker-like pants and a tight fitting rash-guard shirt. His muscles, honed from years of sailing, were prominently displayed through the thin fabric.

"What do you mean, 'do I like it'? It's a beautiful boat. You win races with that kind of boat," I answered.

"Good. She's yours." Robbie watched my expression carefully as shook my head, trying to figure out exactly what he meant.

"You're giving me a boat?"

"Yes. I figured it's the least I could do. I knew you could always use something to race in, so I thought this would work. Do you like it?" A hint of concern that I might turn him down entered his voice, but he did his best to keep it hidden.

He needn't have worried. This was the boat of my dreams.

"This is almost too nice, Robbie. I don't know what to say," I said, stepping closer to the beautiful work of art that was this boat.

"Yes. You should say yes. It's not like I can't afford it."

"Then yes. And a big, big thank you," I said. His face relaxed as I smiled. "How did you know I would want this one? She's perfect."

Robbie blushed slightly. "I saw that you placed with this boat at nationals last year. You got your best times with this model."

"This has always been my favorite." I grinned and gave him a hug. His body pressed into mine, and I felt something in the pit of my stomach start to heat. I liked the way he felt against me. I held on for a moment longer than necessary, pulling away reluctantly. He just felt so good.

"You want to take her out for a spin?" Robbie's green eyes glinted in the sun with excitement.

"Hell yes! I was wondering how long you were going to make me wait," I said, hopping onto the deck and starting to untie the lines. Robbie laughed, his smile shining across the boat as he untied the mooring lines and jumped aboard.

He went to the back of the boat, taking control of the helm while I started the engine. The motor whirred to life and Robbie navigated us out of the harbor and into deeper waters. The wind was crisp and cool, the dark blue water calm with the white tips of the waves beckoning us out toward the horizon. It was a perfect day for sailing.

I killed the motor once we were far enough from shore, and together Robbie and I prepped the sails. We faced into the wind, and on Robbie's command, I raised the mainsail. Robbie shouted encouragement as I winched the sail to the proper tension, making it tight and tall into the sky.

The smaller, triangular jib went up next, unfurling and ready to catch the wind. Robbie flashed me a grin, turning the boat so that the sails filled with wind. The boat surged with power, coming alive and dancing across the water.

It felt wonderful to be working with him, the two of us shouting out what we were doing and what needed done. The two of us worked together seamlessly as if we had never been apart, urging the boat faster and faster.

The boat handled like a dream, increasing in speed and almost seeming to guide the wind into her sails. She cut through the ocean, the water dancing with life around her bow. Spray rose up and glittered through the air, catching the sun like falling jewels. It was a dream come true to sail such a perfect boat and know that she was all mine.

After a time, Robbie steered back into the wind, and the boat slowed to a stop. I pulled the sails down, tossing the sea anchor into the water. The blue sea sparkled like a giant sapphire as we stopped in the middle of the ocean, the shore line barely visible in the distance. It was something we used to do when we were kids, stopping to talk where no one could hear us, and I was glad he remembered it.

Once everything was secure, we both sat on the deck and Robbie pulled out a Snickers for the two of us to share. I kicked off my shoes, feeling the warm deck on my bare feet. Robbie's face concentrated as he carefully tore the bar into two fairly equal halves and let me pick. The sweet chocolate and caramel tasted fantastic as we sat in the sun.

"So, why aren't you out sailing professionally? I saw you were scheduled for some Olympic qualifying events, but that you didn't race," Robbie asked, his mouth full of chocolatey goodness.

"Have you been following my racing career, Robbie Saunders?" I asked. He blushed slightly.

"Maybe a little."

"My teammate had a back injury and couldn't race. Then when everything happened with Avery's grandmother and I needed to move out to be with Grace, I just took the season off." I shrugged as if it weren't a big deal.

Robbie examined me, his green eyes seeing right through my nonchalance. "I see."

"It sucks, but I didn't really have much of a choice. No

partner, and Avery needed me," I tried to explain, but his expression didn't change.

"So why don't you sail single-handed? I remember you used to be pretty good at it. If you need a sponsor, I'll do it. I sponsor other racers all the time." He licked the last of the chocolate off his fingers, and I had a hard time not focusing on his perfectly shaped mouth.

"I don't sail single-handed. It's just not something I enjoy anymore. And Grace needs me to watch Avery now. I just don't have the availability."

"I could throw in a nanny as part of your sponsorship," he said.

"You do that for all your racers?" I teased, hoping he would drop it. I didn't like sailing single-handed. Despite everyone's insistence, I knew my parents died because I was out sailing by myself. It was sailing single-handed that led to their deaths.

"Just the ones I like. I'm serious, though. You should be sailing, Sam." Robbie leaned back, stretching his legs out in front of him. The sun caught his sandy hair, and he looked like an angel. But despite the fact that in that moment he was a gorgeous specimen of a man, I wasn't going to let him pressure me into sailing by myself.

"No, Robbie. Thank you, but I won't do it. Please don't push. I sail double-handed. Two people. That's it."

"Okay." A smile crossed his face, and I knew he wasn't going to try anymore. Robbie was stubborn, but he knew I could out-stubborn him. "So what do you want to name your boat?

I thought about it for a moment, frowning slightly as I went over names. It needed to be something special; something to do with family and the chance at making things better. "Let me think for a bit."

Robbie nodded. "You got it."

"Hey," I said, pointing to the distance. "Dolphins!"

"There's a pod that lives around here. They've always brought me good luck whenever I see them before a race." Robbie shielded his eyes and looked out across the water. The acrobatic creatures leapt through the waves, twisting and turning like dancers. I envied their grace through the water, the ability to sail without needing a mast.

I followed the dance of the dolphins as they disappeared into the ocean behind us. A sassy grin spread across my face as I stepped to the aft, looking down into the water.

"Hey, Robbie! Come look at this fish! I've never seen anything like it," I called out. There was no fish. There never was a fish, but Robbie used to fall for it every time. I hoped he would fall for it again.

"What? Coming," he answered. I heard him stand and pad softly across the deck to the stern. He came up beside me and peered into the blue sparkling water. "I don't see it..."

I pushed his shoulders, toppling him into the water. He landed with an ungraceful splash, spluttering and spitting out saltwater as he surfaced.

"Oh, it's a Robbie fish!" I bit my lip for a moment, hoping he wasn't angry, but his laughter soon filled my ears.

"Ha, ha. Very funny." He stuck is tongue out at me as he treaded water. His shirt had gone transparent, and I could very clearly see every one of his deliciously defined muscles.

"Come help me up," he said, motioning me toward the water. I went to my knees, laughing that he had fallen for my joke yet again, and offered him my hand. His wet fingers clasped strongly around mine, and I suddenly realized what I had just done. I couldn't believe I had forgotten this part. He flashed me an evil grin and pulled down hard, toppling me into the ocean.

The water was cold and incredibly salty. I was very glad I had kicked off my shoes and was wearing light clothing, but even though I was a strong swimmer, it was still hard to stay afloat. I surfaced, and Robbie was laughing, his head bobbing gently above the dark water.

"You fall for it every time," he snickered. I splashed a handful of water at him.

"You fell for it first." I ducked as he returned fire with a splash of his own. I couldn't stop giggling as we attempted to splash one another, darting around the water like dolphins ourselves.

My watch started to beep. I gave it an evil glare, but it didn't stop its high-pitched chirps. Robbie's expression went quizzical, and I sighed.

"I have to get home. Avery gets out of school in an hour and I have to pick her up." I wished I could just stay out on the boat for the rest of the day. That I could sit in the sunshine with the cool breeze on my face and enjoying Robbie's company forever. Instead, I needed to go brave the traffic of a million soccer moms and their rebellious progeny.

"All right, let's get those sails back up," Robbie said, reaching for the boat. He lifted himself easily out of the water, offering me a hand back up on deck. His hand was warm and strong against mine as he hauled me up. There was no way I would have been able to pull him into the water.

I stumbled up onto the deck, and he caught me in his arms. He was so close, his body warm even after being in the ocean. I looked up into his green eyes and my body pressed into him of its own volition.

My watch beeped again, reminding me that I had someplace I needed to be. The moment was broken, and he turned away. I silently cursed myself for wanting to kiss him. He was Robbie, my best friend. But he was also so much more now than he was eleven years ago.

He walked effortlessly across the boat, moving as though he had been born on the water. He hauled the sea-anchor up, his muscles flexing under his shirt. My mouth watered a little at the sight of him. Robbie was no longer the boy I had sailed with. He was a man and a good looking one at that.

I hoisted the sails and we hurried back to the docks, making good time. The wind had shifted, and it made our trip back easy. The wind was cold against my wet skin, but between the breeze and the sunshine, I'd dried out enough not to be worried about the cold. I was suddenly very glad the day had been almost unseasonably warm. As the dock came into view, Robbie switched on the engine, and I took down the sails. Robbie steered us easily into the slip, and I had the boat-hook and ropes ready to tie the boat down.

It only took us a moment to secure the boat, the knots flowing from our fingers as we tied and secured everything. Robbie did a quick double-check before we jumped from the boat and onto the dock.

"You are covered in salt," Robbie said, laughing as he brushed white grains from my cheek. "There's a freshwater bucket over there."

He took my hand and guided me toward an old-fashioned water spigot and turned it on. Crystal clear water sloshed out, and I put my hand under the flow. The water was warm, and I smiled. Robbie lifted a bucket and slid it under the spout. Memories of the last time the two of us had rinsed off under a bucket like this flooded my mind. I found myself aching to kiss him.

Robbie raised the bucket over my head, his strong arms steady as he prepared to pour it. I stepped in close to him, and he let the water fall over us. I stood on tiptoe and found his lips with mine, the water cascading around us.

This kiss wasn't the innocent first taste of love between two friends. Robbie didn't freeze this time, no longer a boy unsure of oncoming masculinity. This time, he let the bucket fall, his fingers tangling in my hair as he pressed his lips against mine. His body met mine, his heat seeping through wet clothes and filling me with a fire of want. Our tongues met, the taste of freshwater mixing in with the kiss. It was sweet and clean and everything I had ever expected in a kiss.

My watch beeped again, giving me one final warning. Breathless, I pulled away, our foreheads still touching as our lips separated.

"Go pick up your niece. I'll finish up here." Robbie's voice was low and full of want. Our eyes connected, and I lost myself in his sea of green for a moment.

"Okay," I replied. My head was spinning. I wondered if I had forgotten how to breathe. I stepped back, and Robbie's hands went to my shoulders. He looked me up and down and smiled.

"Thank you for the boat," I whispered. I leaned forward and kissed him again, not ready to leave him just yet. His mouth caressed mine, and time stopped for a moment. Then he pushed me back gently.

"You better go or you'll be late," he said. His green eyes held a fire that said he didn't want me to go, that he wanted so much more. I fought inwardly with myself, but I knew I had to leave.

"*Avery's Hope*," I said, taking a step back. His brows came together in a question. "I want to name the boat, *Avery's Hope*."

Robbie nodded. "That's a perfect name; and I think Avery will approve."

I took another step backward, making the distance between us grow and hoping that the extra space would make it easier to leave him. It didn't, but I knew I couldn't stay. I turned and started to walk back down the pier, my fingers going to my lips to feel the passion still surging within them.

"Hey, Sam?" Robbie called out. I turned, ready to run back down and into his arms if he asked. "I'd like to see you again. Can I take you out to dinner tomorrow?"

I beamed at him. "Yes. I get off of work at four."

"Excellent. I'll be at your house at five then. Dress fancy." His smile lit up the dock brighter than the sun. I nodded enthusiastically and then forced myself to hurry away so I could get to Avery by the time school got out.

CHAPTER 10

The coastal town of Winchester was not that big. It was a really nice tourist town, with a big, beautiful marina, three restaurants, and a bar that is more local than tourist. Technically, Grace and I didn't even live within the town's limits, but the sheriff still looked after us like we did.

New York City was about an hour away by train, so if any of the small town's inhabitants wanted to treat someone or have a night out, most of them usually hopped on the train. Unless, of course, they happen to be the son of a billionaire.

It was just before five, and Robbie was right on time. I peeked out the window and nearly didn't recognize the man walking up. I still saw him in my mind as the gangly, awkward twelve-year-old boy who liked wearing basketball shorts and t-shirts. I had only ever seen him in sailing gear or khakis since we became adults, and I was surprised to find he even owned a suit.

Where I was expecting a sailor, a prince stood on my front porch. He had tamed his wild sandy hair into something that could grace the cover of a men's magazine, and his normally scruffy chin was clean-shaven. A black suit jacket hung perfectly across his broad shoulders, and a dark green shirt underneath it made his green eyes pop. A tie was never his style, so I wasn't surprised not to see one, but even without it, he looked ready to go to dinner with a movie star.

I gulped and let the curtain fall. I felt almost too casual in my dark blue dress, but it was the nicest thing I had. I knew it looked good, but it was my go-to dress for weddings, banquets, award ceremonies, and anything that needed me to wear something fancier than jeans. Seeing Robbie looking like the billionaire he was, my dress suddenly felt a little shabby. I smoothed the front and made sure my hair was still pulled back. Grace and Avery had enjoyed teasing it into curls and doing my makeup. Even if my dress was a little plain, my hair and face more than made up for it.

"I GOT IT!" screamed Avery as the doorbell chimed. She tore down the hallway, her princess dress flowing behind her, and threw open the door before I even had a chance to move. She loved answering the door.

"Hi," Robbie greeted her, bending down and resting on his heels to be at her eye level. "I am supposed to take a princess to dinner tonight. You look ready to go."

Avery beamed up at him, twirling her iridescent princess skirt at her feet. It was supposed to be her Halloween costume, but she refused to wear anything else. It was a struggle in the mornings to convince her to wear her school uniform, and she only changed when Grace promised she could wear her princess costume as soon as she got home. Halloween was still over a month away, but she wasn't showing any signs of getting bored with it.

"Aunt Sam, there's a man at the door for you," Avery called out, her eyes never leaving Robbie. I could tell she was smitten, and given how handsome he looked in that suit, I couldn't blame her.

"Thank you, Avery," I said, walking over to the open door. Robbie's jaw dropped slightly.

"Wow... you look amazing..."

Heat flared through my cheeks, and I put my hands on Avery's shoulders just so they had something to do. "Thank you."

"Avery, come here and let your aunt get out the door," Grace's soft voice came from inside the house. She stepped into the hallway with a disapproving look. I wasn't sure if it was meant for Avery or Robbie.

"Grace, it's always nice to see you." Robbie nodded politely at my older sister. "You and your mom have a nice night, okay, Princess?"

Avery grinned up at him, and slowly turned back toward her mother. I picked up my purse by the door, and stepped out into the cooling evening air. I waved to Avery and shut the door firmly behind me. Robbie's hand reached for mine as soon as I released the handle. His skin was warm and rough with calluses, but it fit in mine like it had been designed to go there.

"Did I mention you look amazing?" Robbie asked, guiding me out of the driveway and toward the park near our house. I realized that there wasn't a car parked nearby, but I let him lead the way.

"Yes, thank you. You look pretty good yourself." I squeezed his hand, and he chuckled.

"I wanted to make this evening special. I wanted to look my best for you," he said, turning to glance at me. His green eyes caught the light and sparkled. His smile was beaming and meant only for me. The butterflies in my stomach flapped harder as he smiled at me, and I felt like giggling.

The leaves rustled gently, as the moon started her graceful rise. The oncoming night hummed with magic, the dancing leaves and the glow of the moon promising an evening to remember.

"Where are we going? Did you bring a car?" I asked, glancing around. We were almost to the end of our short block, but there wasn't a car in sight.

Robbie laughed and tugged gently on my hand. "We're almost there."

He led confidently as we rounded the corner, heading toward the small park that Avery liked to play in. As we turned, I could see a helicopter waiting in the middle of the soccer field. I had a sneaking suspicion that we weren't taking the train.

"Is that yours?" I asked as we came closer.

"No, it's my brother's, but he said I could use it for the night." He laughed when I gave him a doubting look. "No, I really did ask! It's all ours for the evening."

A wave of excitement washed over me as Robbie led me to the door and helped me inside. I had never been on a helicopter before. Robbie handed me a set of headphones, placing a matching set on his ears as he sat down next to me. The whir of the blades thundered above us as the pilot began to take off.

I gripped Robbie's hand, peering out the window as the ground floated away. There were no jumps or a speeding sensation like there was with a plane, just the ground disappearing below us. I grinned at Robbie, mesmerized by the way the trees shrank and the world suddenly stretched out before me. I liked flying in a helicopter.

The time flew by quicker than I thought it would and before I knew it, we were coming in for a landing on the top of the DS Oil and Gas building. I pressed my nose to the glass, seeing the city for the first time. Despite being so close, I hadn't had a reason to visit New York City yet. I couldn't believe how big it was!

We landed with a simple thump, and Robbie grinned, helping me out of the helicopter, his hand warm in mine. I was glad he didn't let go as he ushered me quickly across the rooftop and down into the building.

"That was spectacular! I could see the whole world from up there," I said in amazement. We stepped into a gold-plated elevator. Robbie pushed the button for the garage, and I leaned back against the shiny cage. I still held onto Robbie's hand, though.

Robbie grinned. "If you liked that, then you'll love dinner."

"Where are we going for dinner?" Curiosity bubbled up inside of me. There were so many fabulous places to eat in New York City, but something that related to a helicopter ride?

"You'll see when we get there," Robbie said with a smug smile.

"You aren't going to tell me?" I gave him my best pout.

"Nope. I like being able to surprise you," he said, his tall frame coming in close to mine. I could smell his cologne and the clean scent of his shampoo. The aroma was intoxicating and wonderful. His lips were so close, all I had to do was rise up on my toes just a little, and I could kiss him. I started to lift up, my mouth inching ever closer to his, when the elevator dinged and the doors opened. Robbie gave me a wicked smile and pulled away, grabbing my hand and tugging me out the elevator doors.

A sleek, black sedan was ready for us, a driver waiting with open doors at the curb. I followed Robbie, my heels clicking on the cement. The interior was warm and spacious and smelled of leather and new car. As soon as we were situated, the car pulled out smoothly into the New York evening.

Buildings rose up into the night sky, their lights twinkling like stars. It was as if each skyscraper were its own universe, full of twinkling galaxies of light, and together they created heaven. Robbie leaned back in his seat, a small smile on his lips as he watched me take in the city. I couldn't look away from the towering buildings and the people hurrying in mass numbers across the busy sidewalks. I had never seen so many people at once, especially in the evening. I could easily see why New York was called the city that never sleeps.

The car came to a gentle stop in front of a spectacular building and Robbie helped me out and onto the curb. The air was colder than I had expected, and I shivered slightly. Robbie's brow creased for a moment, and he quickly shrugged out of his jacket, draping it around my shoulders. It was warm from his body and surrounded me with a scent that was only his. With quick confident steps, he hurried me out of Times Square and into a hotel. I gave him a concerned look, as I wasn't quite ready to just hop into a hotel room at that point. I wanted to kiss him again like crazy, but my sister would kill me if she found out we went straight up to a hotel room. He just grinned and pulled me into an elevator and hit the forty-eighth floor button.

The elevator rose smoothly, and I slid my hand into his. His callused fingers surrounded mine, warm and strong. It only took a moment before the doors opened out into a beautiful restaurant with giant windows. It was quite possibly the most stunning thing I had ever seen.

The hostess greeted us and hurried us to a table for two next to one of the big pane-glass windows. The lights from the city twinkled like fireflies in the dark, the Empire State Building directly in front of us. Robbie pulled out my chair before sitting across from me. The sounds of tinkling laughter and playful chatter filled the restaurant as the guests enjoyed themselves.

"This is amazing," I whispered, looking out the window and seeing the buildings shift. I realized the floor moved slightly and the view changed as the entire restaurant slowly rotated.

"It's moving!" I gasped, and my eyes went wide. Robbie laughed and reached across the table to take my hand. I was glad, because I really didn't ever want him to let go. Even just the short time apart between him pulling out my chair to that moment seemed too long to not touch him.

"It will make a full 360° turn every hour. This way, you'll be able to see the whole city and still get dinner," Robbie said. His green eyes danced with mirth, and I couldn't look away from his smile. *Screw the city,* I thought, *I've got the best view.*

"Good evening. Can I interest you in a wine flight? Or perhaps some champagne to get the evening started?" a waitress asked. She was beautiful, with long blonde hair, blue eyes, and legs that went on for miles. I instantly felt distrust toward her for being so effortlessly beautiful, but I did my best to smile back.

"I'd love some champagne. Dom Perignon Rose if you have it, please," Robbie said. He gave her a quick smile before looking back at me.

"Of course. I'll be right back with that," the waitress cooed, placing her hand on Robbie's shoulder. He didn't even look at her; he just kept smiling at me until she left.

"I hope you don't mind that I ordered for you. It's one of

my favorites," he said. His thumb stroked the palm of my hand, sending thrills up and down my spine.

"No, it's fine. I don't know anything about champagne, so I'm glad you did. This is all so fancy--I have no idea what to order," I said sheepishly, looking down at the menu. Lobster, filet mignon, lamb, and mussels with delicious sounding descriptions all stared up at me.

"I recommend the steamed mussels in Normande sauce. The brandy in the sauce gives it a sweetness that is just perfect," he suggested. I giggled.

"You are just trying to get me in the mood," I teased. "Dinner in a luxurious hotel, now suggesting an aphrodisiac for dinner..."

"You're thinking of oysters, but if that's what you want, then I won't say no." He gave me a naughty wink, and I felt a blush sear across my cheeks. The corners of his eyes crinkled slightly as he chuckled.

"Champagne?" the pretty waitress interrupted, batting her long eyelashes at Robbie. He nodded patiently for her to open and pour the bubbly liquid. I couldn't imagine a more overt sexual innuendo as she held the bottle and popped the cork, her mouth open and the look of pleased surprise almost inappropriate. The smile on my face became wooden. She was much more attractive than I was. Her long, blonde hair was curled and her dress looked expensive. My straight hair was losing the curls Grace and Avery had managed to coerce hours ago, and I knew my dress was far less revealing than hers.

But Robbie didn't seem to notice. Once the champagne was poured, he listed off his order with polite words, and as soon as he finished, he took my hands in his and smiled. The blonde pouted, but she very clearly got the message that he wasn't interested in her. He was interested in me. A rush went through me, and the smile on my face became genuine again.

"So, tell me, what happened after you moved away? All of it. I tried calling you a couple of times, but the call never went through," Robbie asked, his attention solely on me. It was hard to concentrate with his green eyes absorbing my every detail, and the warmth from his hands seeping into mine and filling my core.

"Well, we moved to Texas to start Dad's new company idea. Things looked good for a while, but then everything kind of fell apart. Dad's business partner stole some funds, and then the creditors came knocking." I shrugged. "We moved a lot. He was actually thinking of reapplying for his old job at DS Oil and Gas when the accident happened."

"I heard about that. I was really sorry that happened; I liked your parents," he said softly with a gentle squeeze for my hands.

"I don't really like talking about it. Thank you, though." I took a deep breath and continued, "Anyway, I moved into Grace's apartment after that. She got married and had Avery a couple years after that, and sailing picked up."

"So why are you in Winchester, then?" he asked. His face was so concerned and interested in my well-being, I almost didn't want to tell him what had happened. I didn't really like talking about my past, and I was actually surprised I had said as much as I had. It was a testament to Robbie that he could get me to tell him any of it.

"The house was Avery's grandmother's. When Avery's dad Evan died, Grace and Avery moved in with Evan's mom, Betty. She died in the spring, and so I came out to help raise Avery." I took a sip of my champagne.

"And that's why you're not sailing, right?" Robbie asked. I nodded.

"That and Cora's injury. I hope I can get back next season, but it's going to be rough." I shrugged, trying to make it appear as though I didn't care. Taking this season off was almost certainly death for my career, but I hadn't seen any way out of it.

"We have to get you back out on the water," Robbie said. His eyes went serious for a moment. "Have you ever heard of the Champion of Champions Invitational in Chicago? It's a freshwater event, but it's the last race of the season."

"Have I heard of it?" I made an incredulous noise. "I've wanted to race it for years. It's super prestigious, though, and there is no way I could get in..." I stopped and stared at him. "You have an invite, don't you?"

"Get one every year," he said and sipped on his champagne like it was nothing. "I usually don't even go because I don't like to race double-handed, but for you, I would."

"You'd race with me?" I studied his face. Robbie Saunders never raced double-handed. He only ever did single-handed events. In every interview where they asked him why he raced single-handed, he said he never had a partner he could trust.

"For you, Sam. Yes."

I sat back in my chair, floored. This wasn't something that he took lightly. This wasn't something I took lightly. For him to offer to sail with me, to give me the chance at the Champion of Champions Invitational was a big deal. It was the opportunity of a lifetime to even sail in the race, but the idea of sailing with Robbie was what had me more excited.

"Let's do it." Our eyes met and Robbie smiled.

"I thought you'd say that. It's in two weeks, so I'd like to get some practice time in with you before we race," said Robbie.

I nodded. "I'll have to clear it with Grace. She's in the

middle of school, and I'll have to find someone to watch Avery, but... thank you, Robbie."

He gave me a soft smile that made me want to kiss him. He must have known how much losing this season had hurt, as only another sailor could. It had broken my heart not to race and the idea that I would be racing in the race of my dreams was almost too much to bear.

"You are most welcome."

I would have stood up and kissed him right there, in front of the whole restaurant, but at that moment our food arrived. As soon as the meal was in front of me, I realized I was starving. Robbie shared a bite of his filet mignon with me in exchange for one of my mussels.

The meal was perfect. The food was delicious and the view outstanding, but the best part was Robbie's company. Robbie and I talked into the night, laughing and sharing stories as we caught up on one another's lives. It was the first time in a long time that I felt completely happy and content while not on the water.

"What about your sailing, Robbie? I saw you did well this year," I said, chewing slowly on a mussel and enjoying the flavor. He shrugged and took a sip of his champagne before answering.

"I plan on entering another World Cup next year. I came close to winning, but I sat out during the storm. If I had sailed through it, I would have placed this year. Live and learn," he answered. "What about you?"

"My sponsors say that I'll *probably* be able to race for them next season. I'll have to find a new racing partner, but I'm still hopeful that it will work out. If I'm lucky, this season off won't ruin my chances for next year." I paused and took another bite of food. "If things fall through though, I'll just take a position with a sailing school. I've always wanted to teach."

"You'd be a good teacher." He gave me a level look. "You'd have to make sure the students actually follow the rules, though."

I laughed. "That's why I always liked sailing with you, Robbie. You made sure I didn't do stupid stuff. And you're good at explaining things; you'd make a fantastic teacher too."

"Teaching?" he scoffed. "I don't know. I guess maybe someday, but for now, I just want to race."

I nodded. I took a sip of champagne and smiled to myself. I could see Robbie teaching someday and being amazing at it. In my opinion, he'd be an even better teacher than racer, and he was already one of the best racers I knew.

~

"Can I interest you in a second bottle of champagne?" the waitress asked, giving Robbie a toothy smile. We had just finished dessert, and I was stuffed. There was no way I could drink or eat anything else. An introspective smile crossed his face and he shook his head.

"No, thank you. One is more than enough tonight."

The waitress got a confused expression on her face. The notorious Robbie Saunders who liked to drink would have been on his third or fourth bottle by now. "Are you sure?" she asked.

"Yes. I think this one was more than enough. Thank you. I think we're actually finished," he replied politely, handing her his credit card. She left and he looked at me, his smile telling me he was rather proud of himself. "Do you know the last time I only had one drink at a restaurant? I think you might be a good influence on me, Sam."

"I always was," I managed to answer with a straight face. Robbie laughed.

"That's not how I remember it. If I recall, you were the one who convinced me we could parachute off the roof. It's a good thing I wanted to do a test flight before we actually did it!"

I laughed, remembering his serious little face at how we had to have a pre-flight checklist and a test run. It was a good thing we practiced on the trampoline before jumping off the roof. Mr. Saunders caught us jumping on the trampoline with our ridiculous backpacks stuffed with bed sheets and made sure Robbie and I didn't break all the bones in our bodies. It was a good memory.

The waitress returned with Robbie's card, and touched his shoulder before leaving. A surge of jealousy rippled through me, but he didn't even smile at her as he signed the receipt and pocketed his card.

"You ready? I know Grace wanted you home before midnight." His smile was only for me. He stood and offered me his hand. I took it gladly.

"I don't think she'll mind if we're a little late. I've never been in the city before, and I'd love to walk around a little if that's okay?" I smiled as he wrapped his jacket around my shoulders. His hand pressed into the small of my back as he guided me to the elevator.

"Whatever my lady wants," he replied with a grin as the elevator door opened and we stepped inside. I leaned against him in the empty elevator, feeling his warm body hard against mine, his arm wrapped around me with his hand still on my back. The doors glided shut, and I couldn't help myself. I stood up on my toes and kissed his cheek. I had wanted to kiss him again all night.

His face was warm and smooth, shaved clean for our date. I caught the corner of his mouth with my lips, feeling it curl up into a smile.

"If you're going to kiss me, I'm going to need more than that," he murmured, placing his hand on my neck and pulling me into him. His lips were hot and urgent against mine, his tongue sweet and insistent. I drank him in thirstily, like he was water in the desert.

The door chimed as the elevator came to a stop. Robbie pulled back, breathless and flushed. His green eyes burned like fire and he flashed me a fantastic grin. I couldn't wait to kiss him again. The doors opened, and we strolled out into the lobby of the hotel as if nothing had happened, but there was an extra pep to my step, knowing that I had just kissed the most handsome man in the world.

CHAPTER 11

Outside the night air was almost cold, but in the warmth of Robbie's jacket, it felt wonderful. We stepped out onto the street, the lights making the night seem like day. The neon billboards and TV advertisements made me feel as if I were trapped in a cross-wired, over-lit Christmas tree. Everything seemed to glow or sparkle, and I was amazed at the sheer number of people still out and about at close to midnight.

Robbie wrapped his arm protectively around my waist. I was glad to have him with me. The city was so big, and there were so many people that if he weren't there to guide me, I knew I would have been lost in a moment. It also let me look around, taking in the sights without looking like a complete tourist. I knew with Robbie with me, I could gawk and no one would hassle me.

We walked along the brightly lit street. I knew my eyes were as big as saucers trying to take it all in. Robbie laughed at my childlike interest, pointing out things that he knew I would enjoy. There were signs for Broadway plays, flashing billboards, and beautiful people walking along the street. It was noisy and busy, but I loved taking it all in.

"Where should we go? Do you want to go get a drink somewhere?" I asked, glancing around for a bar or restaurant.

"No, I don't want to drink anything. I'm having a wonderful time just being with you. I'd rather not go into a noisy bar and fight for drinks. I'm much happier just walking with you," Robbie said. He looked almost surprised at his words, but I knew they were true. The arm around my waist tightened as he gave me a loving squeeze and kissed the top of my head.

"I'm having a wonderful time. Thank you for bringing me out." I snuggled up closer to him.

"You are most welcome," he replied. We stopped in front of a window, peering in at the sparkling jewelry inside. "I'd like to buy you something," Robbie whispered.

"You don't have to do that! You already bought me a boat," I told him.

"But you deserve to have more. Would you like that diamond necklace?" He pointed to a beautiful piece of jeweled artwork in the window. It sparkled under the lights and probably cost more than my house.

"It *would* look good with my racing gear..." I mused. Then I punched his arm. "No. I'd never wear it, and it's too pretty to just sit in my jewelry box. Thank you, but no."

"Okay, then. I'd still like to buy you something, though." His eyes were soft as he smiled. We continued to walk down the street.

"But I don't want anything. You've got me into the Invitational. What more could I possibly ask of you?" I asked. "Except to maybe go in that toy store with me..."

Wide open doors of a store beckoned customers into a

shop full of childhood wonder. I could see thousands of toys inside. I was always on the lookout for something to spoil Avery with, and since the money from the accident was in my bank account, I felt like I could actually afford to get her something.

Robbie laughed an, "Of course!" and together we walked into the gleaming toy store.

The store was amazing. Toys, books, games, costumes, and beautiful colors filled the shop. There was a golden castle big enough for Robbie and me to walk through, and a replica of the Empire State Building with working lights. Glowing plastic trees and whimsical designs accentuated the feeling of being in a magical world made especially for children.

Robbie let go of me and picked up a hardcover children's book. His eyes misted over as he flipped through the pages, suddenly lost in his own world. He turned a page, tracing a finger along the drawing of a cartoon stuffed bear.

"There was a picture of Rachel reading this book to Jack and me on Dad's nightstand the night before he died." He turned the page, a smile curling the corners of his lips in soft remembrance. "I used to love this book."

I stepped closer, peeking over his shoulder. He brushed the picture on the page with reverence, and I knew he wasn't reading the book so much as remembering it.

"I would 'read' it to anyone who would listen." He looked up, making eye contact with me for the first time since we entered the store. "I couldn't actually read it, but I had the words memorized. Dad used to sit me on his lap and listen to me on nights he came home from the office."

I tucked my arm under his, leaning my head against his shoulder as he continued to thumb through the pages of his beloved book. I rarely got to see this side of Robbie.

"Your dad sure loved you," I said quietly. Robbie stiffened and closed the book, setting it back on the shelf.

"You sure?" His voice was cold and distant. "Just because he let me read some book to him... it doesn't mean anything."

"Robbie," I said softly. "I know he did. I saw it."

"You weren't there when it changed. After you left, it was all about Jack and the company. DS Oil and Gas was more of a son to him than I was. I got tired of the amount of times I heard him say, 'Why can't you be more like your brother and work for the company?'" Robbie shook his head and pulled away from me, heading deeper into the store.

I sighed. I knew the death of his father was still weighing heavily on him, but I had no idea how to make him feel better. I knew his father had loved him. His father had taken the two of us sailing and I had seen the love Daniel had for his son. I just wished there was a way to make Robbie see it too.

I hurried after him, catching up to him by a small tower of blocks.

"I'm sorry, Robbie. I didn't mean..."

"No, it's not your fault. I don't really want to talk about my dad right now though, okay?" His eyes held a depth of grief that made my heart ache. He took a deep breath and forced a smile. "Let's see what's in that castle over there."

I followed him, letting him lead me to an opulent golden castle filled with all kinds of princess paraphernalia. Pink and purple dominated, and I chuckled to myself. If Avery were here, she would have thought she had died and gone to heaven.

"Oh... My.... Gosh..." I said, staring at a row of the most amazing princess costumes I had ever seen. There were dozens of them, each in a different style and color. Every one of them was something that Avery would have committed murder with a gleeful look on her face to get.

"Isn't Avery going through a princess phase? The couple of times I've seen her, she's been wearing that princess costume," Robbie asked, following me as I looked at the dresses. I wanted to get her one so badly, but some of the dresses cost over a hundred dollars. I started looking for one that was more in my price range, flipping through the tags and trying to ignore the most elaborate ones.

"To say she is obsessed would be an understatement. It's a fight every morning to get her out of the costume and into her school clothes. She snuck out yesterday with the costume on under her uniform," I replied. I pulled out a beautiful golden ball gown, but made a face when I saw the price tag. Just because I was now financially okay didn't mean I should spend that much money on something so frivolous.

Out of the corner of my eye I saw Robbie walk over to a sales clerk and point toward the dresses. I groaned a little inwardly. If the clerk came over, I would be pressured to buy one of the more expensive ones. I turned back to the rack, hoping that she wouldn't actually come and try to help me.

"Hello, what size is the little girl you are buying these for?"

Crap, I thought, but I turned around and smiled politely.

"Well, my niece is five years and tends to fit the small size for most things," I said. I kept going through the rack, hoping I could find something less than fifty dollars.

"Excellent. Thank you," the woman replied, turning and then heading back to the counter. That was not the response I had been expecting. I frowned slightly and looked at Robbie. He was leaning against the clerk's checkout counter, a self-satisfied smirk filling his face. His green eyes danced with amusement. I stopped looking at the dresses and walked up to him.

"What did you just do?"

He puffed up like a satisfied peacock with a cocky grin.

"Robbie..." I put my hands on my hips and gave him my best no-nonsense look. It worked well on Avery and since he was really just an overgrown child, I hoped it would work on him too. He just grinned even more broadly.

"All right, sir. I have your order ready. It will be shipped and at the little girl's house by tomorrow evening," the clerk said, joining us at the counter.

"I'm really sorry, but what is his order?" I asked the young woman.

"He just got one of every dress we offer. Your niece is a very lucky little girl." She gave me a blinding smile. I didn't even want to think what her commission on this sale might be.

"Robbie, you didn't have to do that," I said once the clerk left to go help another customer.

"I know." His eyes twinkled with delight. "But you love that little girl and you want to see her happy."

"But, Robbie, it's so much money..." I stopped when the numbers in my head hit the thousands as I added it up.

"What good is dating a billionaire if he doesn't spend money on extravagant presents?" he asked. I shook my head at him. It was so easy to forget that he had money.

"Thank you. You didn't have to do that, but thank you," I said, a happy smile replacing my no-nonsense look.

"This will make her happy, and in turn, that will make you happy." He leaned forward and kissed my forehead gently. "I think I'm the one who is getting the best part of the deal."

The lights flickered, and a warning that the store would

be closing soon came across the overhead speakers. Robbie took my hand in his, and together we headed back toward the entrance. About halfway to the doors, I stopped, dropping Robbie's hand and hurrying toward the book display.

Robbie watched me, a look of curiosity transforming into a soft smile as I picked up his beloved children's book and quickly paid for it at a small counter nearby.

"I think she'll enjoy reading this to you," I said as I came back to Robbie, the bag looped over my arm.

We stepped out into the New York night, the lights fabulously bright. It felt like it was still daytime with all the people still rushing about, but my watch said it was just past one in the morning.

"I need to get you home before your sister kills me," Robbie said as he saw me looking at my watch. "She's going to think I'm a bad influence or something for keeping you out so late."

I put my hands on his chest, feeling the warmth of his body through the dark green dress shirt. He reached out and pulled me in to him, one hand behind my neck and the other on my waist. Our lips connected, sweeter than honey, and I melted into him. His kiss was gentle at first but also filled with hunger. Every fiber in my being ached to be with him, to have more than just this kiss in a brightly lit street corner.

He released me, breathless and flushed. I knew I was breathing hard, but I could barely contain myself. I wanted to kiss him all night. Damn getting home! Damn tomorrow! All I wanted was to have him kiss me again.

He smiled, his perfect, supple lips curling up and making his eyes sparkle like the ocean. "Time to get you home," he whispered.

I nodded. *Always the good one,* I thought, but I let him

wrap his arm around me and lead me back to the hotel where a car was waiting to take us to the helicopter.

~

I kissed Robbie the whole way home. I'm sure the helicopter pilot thought we were behaving like love-struck teenagers, but I didn't care. I just wanted to kiss him until my lips were raw and even then, I knew I would want more.

The helicopter landed, and Robbie walked me home. The night was cold and I was glad for Robbie's jacket wrapped around me. His hand was warm in mine as he escorted me to my front porch. I stepped as slowly as I could, trying to make the night last forever. I didn't want it to end. I just wanted to stay, my hand in Robbie's, for as long as I could.

The wooden porch creaked softly as we stepped up onto it. I slid my key in the door, hearing the lock click open. Grace had left a light on in the hallway so I wouldn't come home to a dark house. For a moment, I thought about asking Robbie to come inside, but I knew that was a bad idea. Not bad because I was afraid of what would happen, but bad because I knew Avery would come bounding into my bedroom in the morning. As much as I wanted him, it was just going to have to wait.

I turned from the door, and Robbie's arms wrapped around me. He was bathed in moonlight, his eyes deep green pools that I wanted to dive into and never surface. He smiled, his face somehow growing more handsome right before he leaned forward to kiss me. I melted into his kiss, soaking it up and losing myself to him.

I smiled softly as we separated, my heart pounding wildly in my chest. This had been the best night of my life.

"Goodnight, Princess," Robbie whispered as he let me go, stepping back off the porch. I pushed the door open, gliding into the warm house on happy feet. I peeked out the window, watching him stride down the driveway, a silly-happy grin plastered on his face as he walked under the streetlight. Clearly, he had enjoyed the night as much as I had.

I smiled and locked the door, feeling as giddy as a teenager. I knew there was a grin glued to my face and I didn't want it to go away.

I stepped into the kitchen to grab a glass of water to take to bed and nearly ran over Grace. She was wearing an old tattered robe that was once cream-colored, but was now a faded gray. Several pens stuck out of a messy bun while her reading glasses perched precariously on her forehead. She had a big glass of milk and several oatmeal cookies in her hand. I could tell she was still in full study mode.

"I was wondering when you were going to get home, young lady," she whispered, giving me her best motherly glare. I just smiled at her and went to the cabinet to get a glass. "Did you have a good time?"

"I had a spectacular time," I answered, setting the glass on the counter. "He took me to this amazing restaurant, and then we walked around in Times Square. It was so incredibly wonderful."

"Well, at least he didn't hit you with a boat this time."

I looked up at her in shock. Grace stood in the kitchen, crossing her arms and frowning. She was not happy.

"Grace, that was an accident," I said quietly.

"Right. An accident that nearly got you killed." She punctuated her statement with a sigh and her shoulders sagged as though she were carrying the weight of the world. "I know it was an accident, but you can't expect me to welcome him back with open arms after that."

I wrapped my arms around her, hugging her close to me. I hadn't thought of how hard it must have been on her to have almost lost yet another family member. She smelled of oatmeal cookies and ink.

"You know Robbie would never intentionally hurt me," I whispered.

"I know. I just don't want to see you hurt, period. I can't lose you too, Sam." Grace's eyes met mine, and I could see that their blue depths were full of pain and loss. I hugged her closer, feeling her arms tighten around me as well.

"I won't let that happen," I whispered. I heard her sniffle, and she gave me one more squeeze before letting me go.

"You should get to bed. You have work in the morning." She pushed the glasses back onto her petite nose. "And I have to finish studying for this test. I'll see you in the morning, okay?"

"You got it. I'll make the coffee," I promised. Grace smiled and picked up her glass of milk and cookies and headed back into her room. I watched her go and then headed up to my room to get some sleep myself.

CHAPTER 12

*R*obbie was supposed to be here to pick me up at any moment, but I stood half-naked in front of my closet trying to figure out what to wear. My nerves had me jumping and changing my mind about every article of clothing, and even how I should do my hair.

Just relax! I tried to tell myself, but it wasn't working. *He's just Robbie! He won't care what you're wearing or how your hair looks! You are supposed to be sailing!* I knew I shouldn't care, but after the amazing date in New York City two days ago, I was flustered. I had never liked someone as much as I liked Robbie. He made me feel like anything was possible and that the future could be a wonderful place.

I finally just threw on my favorite sailing leggings and a lightweight long sleeved shirt over my bikini. The bikini part was optional, but I felt prettier wearing it than my normal swimsuit. I stared at the mirror for a moment, trying to figure out what to do with my hair. I finally just gave up and put the long, dirty blonde tresses up in a manageable ponytail. I did, however, put just a touch of lipstick on. Just because I was being sensible didn't mean I didn't have to at least try a little bit.

I had a cute skirt with a flattering top in a bag to change into if I needed something dry, and I tossed a waterproof jacket and my sailing shoes in on top of it. I kept a hairbrush and hair-ties in the pocket of the bag, and other than that, I couldn't think of anything else to bring. Nervous butterflies did the mamba in my stomach, and no matter how much I tried to convince myself that this wasn't a date, the butterflies didn't believe me.

A strong knock on the door told me Robbie had arrived. I slung my bag over my shoulder and hurried to the front door, but it didn't matter. Avery had beaten me to it. She had the door open wide, her new princess dress fluttering in the fall breeze as she waved to Robbie. Robbie grinned at me over her head as I made my way to the door.

"Hi, Robbie! Do you like my dress? I like it. Thank you. You ready to take Aunt Sam on a trip?" she asked him, her sentences blurring together in a long stream of little-girl enthusiasm.

"Avery, sweetie, we're just going to go out for today. The race isn't until next week," I answered, giving her a kiss on the top of the head. Avery's small features frowned, and she opened her mouth to say something, but Robbie knelt down in front of her and whispered in her ear. A knowing smile blossomed across her face, and she nodded emphatically at Robbie.

"Right. I forgot. You guys have a good... *day*." She giggled hysterically at the last word, as though she knew some sort of secret. Robbie shook his head and stood up slowly.

"You look amazing. You ready to go?" he asked. He stood confidently in the door, the wind ruffling his sandy hair. The stubble on his chin was back, but it made him look rugged. I rather liked it.

"Yeah, let me just let Grace know I'm leaving," I said, twisting around to call back into the house. Before I could yell out, Grace came out of the kitchen. She had a high-lighter tucked over her ear and her reading glasses on, so I knew she had been studying.

"Hi, Robbie. You two go have fun," she said, grinning like a Cheshire cat. I narrowed my eyes and glanced from Robbie to Grace to Avery. Last time Grace had seen Robbie, she had not been pleased with him, but now she was all smiles. Something fishy was going on. While Avery had a wild imagination, she didn't get confused *that* easily. Grace didn't stop studying for just anything, and Robbie looked just a tad too confident. Something was up.

"All right, you three, what's going on?"

Grace and Robbie exchanged grins and instantly changed their expressions to look innocent. Avery tried to mimic them, but all she ended up doing was looking like she was going to be sick.

"Nothing! Go, have fun! It was great to see you again, Robbie," Grace said, pushing me gently out the door. Avery giggled.

"You too, Grace. Thanks for all your help," he said with a wink.

"Seriously, guys, tell me what's going on?" I pleaded, but Grace just pushed me harder. Robbie moved out of the door, and before I knew it, the front door was shut with Avery and Grace's giggles muffled behind it. I gave Robbie a ques-tioning look.

"What's going on? What sneaky surprise do you three have planned?" I asked. Robbie just laughed and guided me to the car. It was a cute, sporty little red thing. He took the bag from my shoulder and put it in the back seat before opening the door.

I could see Grace and Avery, their blonde hair shining and petite features smiling like jack-o-lanterns in the window, so I waved. Avery waved back emphatically, almost smacking Grace in the face as Robbie started the engine.

"I'll tell you what's going on when we get there," Robbie said cryptically. He pulled out of the driveway and began racing the little car down the street. The cool air felt wonderful against the warm sunshine and I leaned back and just let Robbie drive. I knew I wasn't going to get answers from him until he was ready to share the surprise.

He turned at the intersection leading to the marina, and instead of making a right, he turned left. I sat up in my seat. "This isn't the way to the marina."

"Nope."

I waited for him to say more, but he just gave me an impish smirk that made me want to hit him. I wondered where we were going that he would turn the wrong way.

"Where are we going?" I demanded, looking out the window at the fall foliage flying by. I never came out this direction, so I had no idea where we were headed.

"Some place fun." He shifted into a higher gear, the hum of the sports car singing in the air.

"Where is this 'some place fun'?" I persisted.

"Some place fun. You'll like it." He smirked.

"Argh! Robbie! Tell me where we're going!" I gave his arm a gentle swat, and he laughed.

"Nope, it's too much fun to get you riled. You're pretty when you're mad," he said. I full-on punched his arm this time. "I promise you'll like it."

I slumped in my seat, crossing my arms and pouting. He laughed and turned onto another road. This one I recognized. It was the road to the small, private airport. Robbie turned the car toward the airfield, a plane starting to emerge on the tarmac. He parked the car next to the jet, popping the trunk and grinning wildly. A worn, blue suitcase emerged from the trunk. *My* worn, blue suitcase.

"So that's what Avery and Grace were up to last night. I knew we didn't need more milk! They had me go to the store to get me out of the house. You had them help you!" I sputtered, not really angry but definitely amazed that Avery had kept the secret all day.

"Yup. Grace packed it for me so this could be a surprise. I'm taking you away for the weekend." A little bit of pride at his ability to surprise me filled his voice. He took my hand in his and led me up to the steps of the jet.

I paused at the bottom of the stairs. "How did you get Grace to agree to this?"

"We had a conversation. While you were at work after our date in the city, I went to talk to her." He kicked at a small rock, sending it flying away from the plane. "I saw the look she gave me when I picked you up. She had every right to be mad at me. I nearly killed you. We had a long discussion and I told her my intentions toward you."

"Which are?"

"I can't tell you or it will ruin the surprise. But they are honorable. Well, mostly." He gave me a sly grin that made me laugh.

"And she's okay with you now?"

"Avery's princess dresses might have helped, but yes, we're good," he said. I let out a sigh of relief that I didn't even know I had been holding. Then it hit me that I was leaving Grace and Avery to get on an airplane.

"But what about Grace and Avery? Grace has a test on Monday, and..."

"Grace said she could handle it. Plus, I got her a babysitter for Sunday evening so she can study. Grace said it was fine. She wanted you to have a good time." Robbie handed my suitcase off to a uniformed man who hurried it off into the plane.

"I am going to kill you both," I said, a grin betraying the obvious lie. This was the best surprise I had in a long time. "So where are we going?"

"I can't tell you if I'm dead," Robbie teased. I gave him a playful shove and he wrapped his arms around me, his body solid and strong. I was happy in his arms. We could be going anywhere, but if I was with him, I didn't care.

"All right, keep your secrets. I'll find out soon enough." I gave him a playful glare, his green eyes laughing. He leaned forward, kissing me gently. I closed my eyes, letting his kiss envelop me. Wherever we were going, I was already in paradise.

"Sir, are you ready to depart?" the pilot asked, sticking his head out of the open plane door. Robbie released me reluctantly, lipstick smeared across his lower lip. He grabbed my hand and together we entered the airplane.

It was easy to forget that Robbie was a billionaire. Stepping onto that airplane, though, I knew I was going to enjoy the perks of dating a billionaire.

Comfortable leather couches sat in cozy positions where I was used to rows upon rows of chairs. A big-screen TV dominated a wall, and I could see a fully-stocked bar. It was like our own little club house. This was what I imagined Air Force One must look like. Only nicer.

I picked a loveseat to sit down on as Robbie stowed his travel bag. An attractive stewardess smiled politely, asking me what I would like to drink. I glanced at Robbie and he nodded for me to get whatever I wanted.

"I'd like a Naughty Shirley Temple, please," I asked. The stewardess cocked her head, confused, and Robbie laughed. He thumped ungracefully into the seat beside me, placing his arm over my shoulder.

"She wants a Sprite with grenadine and vodka," he told the flight attendant. Her eyes lit up and she nodded.

"Anything for you, sir?"

Robbie glanced at me and smiled. "No, I'm good. Thank you."

I snuggled into his arm, the smell of leather and Robbie filling my nose. It was a wonderful scent. He kissed the top of my head gently, a smile caressing his handsome features.

The stewardess was back in a moment, drink in hand. A pink umbrella with a maraschino cherry decorated the glass and I grinned like a kid.

"Thank you. Do you know where we are going?" I asked her, keeping my voice innocent.

She gave me a wide smile and shook her head. "Nope." The lie was obvious, but I didn't push it. Robbie gave me a squeeze with his arm.

"You want to know now, or do you want it to be a surprise?" he asked. The engines began to hum a low, rumbling song as they powered up for takeoff. I sipped my drink and thought about it for half a second. While the surprise would be fun, the anticipation was killing me.

"Now. Definitely now," I answered. He laughed.

"We are going to Key Island in the Caribbean."

I recognized the name. "Isn't that where your brother met his wife?"

"Yup," he said. He brushed a stray strand of blonde hair from my forehead, tucking it gently behind my ear. "We are staying at my friend Owen's place."

My brows creased together. While the name sounded

familiar, I couldn't place it. Just because I read the tabloids to keep tabs on Robbie, didn't mean I actually paid attention to them.

"Owen Parker," Robbie said in response to my questioning look. "He was the best man at Jack's wedding, and he has this amazing place on the beach. It's got its own private dock, so I've been interested in buying it for a long time, and he's actually thinking of selling it to me."

"So it's a working weekend?" I asked, sticking my tongue out at him. He laughed.

"You got me. My secret dream to be a real estate mogul is now out in the open."

"Why is he selling it? It sounds like a great place." I closed my eyes, letting my head rest against Robbie's shoulder. The plane started to move.

"His wife is pregnant with their firstborn. She hates flying, so it's hard to get to the island." He shrugged and kissed my head again, smoothing the hair he'd disturbed with his fingers. "Besides, they are running a bed and breakfast in Iowa, his wife's home state. They are super happy out there, and they don't need to fly out to some lavish beach house."

"Hmm," I murmured. The roar of the engines and Robbie's gentle fingers in my hair were lulling me into a delightful sleepiness. "I think we are going to have a wonderful weekend."

"Me too," Robbie whispered as the plane lifted into the air. "Me too."

CHAPTER 13

The island was more spectacular than I could have dreamed. I kept my face pressed up to the window like a child as the town car drove through the island streets and up to the beach mansion. As the driver pulled into the rounded driveway in front of the impressive house, I pinched the inside of my arm to make sure I wasn't dreaming. Robbie glanced over with a frown at the slight yelping sound I made, but I just grinned at him. This was no dream.

The car parked and I stood in front of the house, just taking it all in. The air was humid and rich with the smell of the ocean and plant life. After the reds and golds of the trees up North, the lush greenness, even in the dark, was almost overwhelming. Night coated the island like a blanket, but spotlights illuminated the big house with white columns and a red tile roof, making it seem welcoming and warm.

"You ready for a nice little cruise before bed?" Robbie asked, taking my hand as I stood looking at the house. I turned toward him, my brow furrowed, and he smiled. "I did promise to take you sailing today."

I laughed. A slight breeze played with my hair, and I felt

the need to be out on the water. It was a perfect evening for sailing; the stars were twinkling brightly in the sky, and the moon was just rising over the horizon. I kissed Robbie's cheek and then took off running.

Robbie was hot on my trail as I followed a small path of sand around the side of the house. I came around the corner and stopped dead in my tracks at the view. The ocean stretched out before me with thousands of stars mirrored in its shimmering depths. Robbie giggled as he dodged past me, running quickly down to the dock. He jumped easily from the small, wooden dock into a suspiciously familiar boat bobbing gently in the dark waves.

I sprinted after him, my steps falling with hollow thuds on the wood out to the boat. I slowed my steps long enough to untie the boat and then leapt aboard *Avery's Hope*. Robbie turned on the engine, carefully guiding us out onto the ocean. I took off my shoes, reveling in the sensation of the sea air across my bare skin and my toes on the deck. My normal sailing shoes were back in my bag at the house, but for now, barefoot was better than any shoes I could have wanted.

The water was dark blue with tips of silver moonlight. The waves caught the sparkles of the stars and the entire world felt like a giant reflective jewel. The air was cool enough to be comfortable and smelled fresh and clean like only open ocean air could. I took a deep breath and the air revitalized me after the long flight.

The shore was a faint line on the horizon when Robbie turned off the motor. I went to prep the sails, but Robbie grabbed my hand instead.

"You ready for dinner?" Robbie's eyes sparkled in the moonlight.

"Dinner?" I asked. I hadn't even realized that I was

hungry, but my stomach suddenly growled an answer for me.

"Wait here," Robbie said, letting go of my hand and ducking down into the hold. I could hear him opening and closing doors and cabinets, so I sat down on the bow of the boat to wait. After a moment, he emerged and sat across from me, setting a platter of food between us. The food was arranged in beautiful patterns that I knew Robbie would never have taken the time to make.

"You had this whole thing planned, didn't you?" I asked, shaking my head.

"Yup," he replied with a cheesy grin. I laughed and peered at the plate, trying to decide what I wanted to eat first. There were fried plantains, jerked shrimp, fresh fruit in neat squares, and little tiny bite-sized versions of what appeared to be key lime pie. I popped one of the pies into my mouth, enjoying the sweet and tangy flavor.

"What else do you have planned?" I picked up a shrimp and ate it slowly; the spices of the jerk seasoning were spicy and delicious.

"Wouldn't you like to know?" Robbie answered with a sly smile. His eyes gleamed in the moonlight. I laughed and kept eating, knowing I would enjoy anything Robbie had in store.

We ate in comfortable silence. The food was delicious and I was hungrier than I had expected. It felt wonderful just to be with Robbie, to have the moonlight and the ocean and only him. The boat rocked gently, caressed by the waves. It was like old times with Robbie, only better. His smile in the moonlight sent my heart to fluttering. Anything could happen out here, and I had high hopes for the evening.

"You were hungry," he observed. He smiled as his eyes

followed my fingers to my mouth as I licked the last of the key lime pie from them.

I giggled and glanced at the plate. Together we had cleaned it to nothing but crumbs, and I was considering using my tongue to get those last little morsels. I felt perfectly full and very content.

"It was delicious. I think those fried plantains might be my new favorite food," I said. Robbie laughed and picked the plate up before rising. With confident steps, he padded down into the galley, and I could hear the clank of the plate against the sink as he took care of putting the dish away.

I stood, rolling my shoulders as I walked to the rail of the boat. The dark water sloshed rhythmically against the hull, and I could feel the tension in my shoulders melting into the night. A small smirk crossed my face as I heard Robbie come up behind me.

"Hey, look down there. I think I see some sort of fish," I said to him, pointing at the navy blue water. He leaned out across the railing, searching the water with his eyes. I felt him stiffen as I pushed his shoulders, but it was too late. He toppled into the water with a splash. "Yup, I definitely see a Robbie-fish!"

"Hey," he spluttered, coming to the surface. "You know, you're supposed to wait at least twenty minutes between eating and swimming!"

I laughed and went to the rear of the boat to push the steps into the water. Robbie swam with strong strokes to meet me.

"Help me up," he dared, reaching up his hand with a grin plastered on his face. I hesitated for only a second, ultimately deciding I should keep with the tradition. He pulled me into the water easily, and I laughed as I went under.

The ocean was as warm as bathwater. I surfaced, kicking

water at him. He raised his arm to block the spray, but then roared and started swimming for me. I shrieked and swam away, kicking my legs and swinging my arms as he chased me through the warm waves.

Robbie was always the faster swimmer, and it was only a matter of minutes before he finally caught me by the aft of the ship. His hand wrapped around my ankle and he dunked me under with a swift downward pull. I shook my head free of the water as I emerged, opening my eyes to find him close enough to kiss. The moonlight caught the gleam in his eye as he pulled me closer to him, holding onto the boat to keep us both afloat.

"Kiss me," I said with just a hint of begging. I licked the salt from my lips. His mouth curved up into a smile and he tipped his head to the side, bringing his lips to mine. His tongue was salty with the ocean water as he tasted me, our lips dancing in the dark. Heat began to burn in my core. I didn't want to wait any longer. I wanted Robbie more than I wanted to breathe.

We broke from our kiss and I climbed up the ladder and back onto the deck of the ship, leaving a trail of water behind me. Robbie was hot on my heels, his hands grabbing the ladder's rungs just as my feet left them. I could sense his eyes on the bottom of my body as I climbed the ladder, and I liked the way that made me feel.

When I reached the deck, I quickly wriggled out of my wet sailing leggings. I tried to pull the skintight shirt over my head, cursing the wet fabric that was now sticking to my body. Just as the fabric was directly over my eyes, I felt a pair of hands run their way up my body. I shivered, the air sucking the heat from my wet skin as his fingers sent shocks of electricity through my body.

I recovered quickly. "Aren't you being a little presumptuous?" I asked, a smile on my lips. I couldn't tell if he could see that I was joking, but the last thing I wanted was for him to stop.

My hands were still stuck in the shirt on my head, and one of his hands moved to the middle of my back. He continued to stroke my skin, his other hand going to the shirt. He lifted it up over one ear and whispered softly in my ear. "I very much doubt that."

His hand moved up to my hands, stilling them and keeping me entangled in the shirt. I felt him move around to the front of me. His hand was still on my back, cradling me as if he were dipping me on the dance floor. His maddening contact was teasing me, and I felt my sense of touch begin to heighten the longer my eyes remained covered.

"You know, I thought about the last day we spent together for a long time," Robbie said.

"Me too," I agreed, surprised I could speak any words at all.

"I'm sorry that it took such a boneheaded move from me for us to get back together, but I feel like this was meant to be."

My heart raced faster and my breath caught in my chest. I thought of that time, eleven years ago, when I had my first taste of Robbie.

He moved closer to me. I could feel the drops of water falling off his shirt and onto my skin. "You stole a kiss from me, and I almost missed my chance to kiss you back. Then you went away, and a piece of me has wanted you ever since. *Pined* for you, even."

The confession was a little startling, but I let his emotions wash over me in waves, afraid to even speak because of the chance of ruining the moment. Maybe I hadn't pined for Robbie Saunders, but I had never forgotten that magical kiss.

I felt him lean in, and in anticipation I parted my lips. I was rewarded with the contact of his lips against mine, a tentative taste, almost as if to test if I were the same as I had been eleven years ago. He backed away, and I felt naked under his gaze, unable to cover myself or even see what he was doing. Then, he suddenly leaned in and kissed me again, this time passionately. His hands wrapped around my midriff, and I felt my body quest for his.

He backed off after a moment of thoroughly kissing me, his hands going to my shirt to help get it off. As he pulled the shirt off my head and I regained my sight, he said, "Let's get this off of you. You look ridiculous."

My jaw dropped, but he just smiled and kissed me again, his laughter sweet against my lips. I worked the shirt off of my hands and wrapped them around his body. I let my fingers grab at the bottom of his shirt, quickly pulling it up, feeling his muscular body underneath. This time, I paused with the shirt covering his eyes.

"Now who looks ridiculous?" I asked him.

He smiled. "I can't see, but I assume it's still you." I laughed, and before I could kiss him again, he swept me up in his powerful arms. He started to walk.

"Guess it's time to see if I really can navigate a boat with my eyes closed. Unless you want to help me get this shirt off my eyes."

I pulled the shirt up so one of his eyes was uncovered. It immediately dilated when it saw my body in his hands. "Good enough," he said as he began to walk. I leaned up and wrapped my arms around the back of his neck, leaning up to a kiss. I had no idea where he was bringing me, but I had a pretty good idea as I felt us begin to move down the stairs to below the deck.

In another moment, I was being laid on the small bed of the living quarters. Robbie straightened back up and removed the shirt the rest of the way, and I watched his muscles work. He looked down at me, appreciating my body.

"You know," he said, "I still have to sleep in that bed. It's very inconsiderate of you to be wearing your wet bathing suit on it."

I laughed again, but quickly pulled my bikini top off. I heard him draw his breath in sharply when he saw my breasts. They were small, and few men had ever seemed to have this kind of reaction, but I took advantage of his surprise to throw the bikini top at him. He and I both laughed as it landed on his shoulder and stuck there. I moved my fingers to my bikini bottom.

"Stop," he said. "I can take care of those."

His fingers moved to his own swim trunks, slowly revealing his manhood. The V-shape of his muscles was so sexy that I could barely stand it. Before I had a chance to really look, though, he got down on his knees at the foot of the bed and started to move his hands up my legs.

My breathing started to quicken as I felt his fingers loop under my bikini bottoms, pulling them down and exposing me. As soon as he had the swimsuit off, he spread my legs open, drinking in the sight of me.

I had been in a plane all day and had just played in the ocean, but he seemed to have no hesitation as he applied his tongue to my tender area.

The pleasure was intense. I had often fantasized about Robbie, but he was better in reality than he had been in my imagination. In my fantasies of Robbie, I had always orgasmed quickly, and I knew it wasn't going to take me long this time.

Robbie was an experienced lover. He managed to keep going at the same pace and pressure, even when I began to buck my hips. My hand went through my hair, and I thrashed like a fish on the end of a line. I wanted him. I wanted the rest of my fantasy to come true, for him to become one with me, and when I thought about that, I crested the final wave to my orgasm. Through the waves of pleasure, I could feel him smile as he continued to attack my clit mercilessly.

Eventually I stopped thrashing enough to look down. His eyes were on me, looking up at me as if asking if I were done. I grabbed a handful of his hair and pulled. "I want you. Now."

He grinned from ear to ear. "Okay, hold on a second." In a flash, he was back up the stairs to above deck.

What the heck? I thought to myself. Long seconds passed as I heard him banging around above me, and then he came down the stairs. I held my hands out, as if to ask what his problem was, when he produced a square wrapper.

"I had some time to prepare, but I couldn't sneak down here to have this ready. I didn't want you to catch me and think I was being '*presumptuous*,'" he said, throwing my word back at me.

I smiled. No man had ever been this thoughtful, so prepared. "Well, I guess I can forgive you."

He laughed and tossed me the condom. Then he knelt on the bed, obviously waiting for me to put it on. *Now he* is *being presumptuous*, I thought.

I sat up, getting a good look at him. He was bigger than I had imagined, and I was ready for anything. I carefully placed the condom on him, gently rolling it down. He felt so solid, so big in my small hand, I could feel myself getting more and more turned on.

"Thank you very much," he said, and I laid back down. He positioned himself over me, and in a moment he was pressing into me. His eyes locked with mine in the faint light, but I closed mine as he went deep inside of me. I ran my hands over his muscular chest, which was still slightly wet from the ocean. I opened my eyes and looked down at his hips, working hard to thrust into me. My fingers ran up his biceps, appreciating muscles that had taken a lifetime to build.

He pushed my legs to one side and then rolled me so that I was laying on my side. He got behind me, and I spread myself gently to let him in. His hand went to my shoulder and grabbed tightly as he explored my inner depths. He kissed my back gently as he rocked in and out of my body.

"Oh, you feel so good, Sam," he whispered in my ear. I started to rock against him gently, and he whispered again. "I love the way that feels." I really enjoyed it that he told me what he liked, so I kept doing exactly that. His fingers ran up and down my body, sending shivers of bliss cascading down my skin.

I pulled away and turned toward him. I pushed his arm so that he was lying on his back, then jumped on him, putting both my hands on his solid chest. He grinned at my energy, and as I lowered my body to join with his, he leaned his head back and closed his eyes.

I began to ride him, to grind against his body. I heard him groan in pleasure, which turned me on even more. Suddenly, he grabbed my ass and began to thrust upward, sending me to new heights. He leaned up and his tongue darted out, touching my nipple. He moved from one breast to the other, tasting me, enjoying them.

After enjoying them, he threw his head back into the bed. His thrusting seemed to get a little frantic. I knew what was coming.

"Yes!" I moaned. I leaned down and flattened myself against his body, then whispered in his ear. "Come for me."

His thrusting became quicker and suddenly I felt him grow larger. I breathed out and moaned softly into his ear. He thrust deeply one last time, followed by an erratic series of smaller thrusts. His fingers tightened around my waist, and I felt myself have a small orgasm, almost as if it had transferred from his body to mine.

For long moments he continued to thrust lazily within me, long past the point where his orgasm must have ended. Then, he relaxed, his breathing still ragged. I looked him in the eye, and we kissed tenderly as he left me.

He pulled the condom off, tying it in a knot before it could make a mess. "You know," he said with a smile, "normally I wouldn't make you sleep in the wet spot, but I'm afraid we got the entire bed wet."

I laughed. "So you're saying that this isn't just your bed?"

Robbie shrugged. "Well, I don't want to be *'presumptuous.'* I don't know where else you'd sleep. Might as well just pretend it's a sleepover."

I smiled, then put my head against his chest. "We do have that big lovely house we can go back to."

"There is a big fluffy bed in the master bedroom that I think you'd enjoy." I loved the way his voice rumbled through his chest. "Besides, no one is steering the boat."

I traced my fingers along his chest, traveling the ravines and rises of his muscles. It was a landscape I wanted to live in forever. He wiggled out from underneath me, standing to dress so he could take care of the boat. He always was the one for the rules.

"I don't think I want you to get dressed," I said, looking pointedly at the boxers in his hand. His mouth curved up in a sly grin as he set them back on the floor.

"It's a good thing the house has a private beach, since I can't seem to find your clothes either." He kicked my swim suit away from the bed.

I laughed, jumping from the bed and dancing past him up to the deck. I had always wanted to sail naked in the moonlight, and we had to get home somehow...

CHAPTER 14

 took a deep breath and smiled. Robbie's chest rose and fell with a relaxing rhythm, his heartbeat pulsing gently in my ear. I felt like I could stay like this forever, wrapped up in Robbie's arms and perfectly happy. The sun peeked over the horizon, filling the room with a glorious golden warmth.

We had enjoyed the rest of the evening, sailing naked and just acting like kids again. When we had arrived at Owen's place, we had been so tired that we barely got the boat tied down before falling into bed together. Now it was morning, and I was ready to get up. Robbie, however, shifted under me, turning his head from the light. I sat up on my elbow and lightly kissed his temple, making him smile in his sleep. With careful movements, I slid out of the soft bed and padded gently across the floor to the open balcony. The salt air caressed my skin; the ocean was calling my name.

I closed the curtains, darkening the room to a soft gray. Robbie snored softly as I tiptoed to the closet and found a long terry-cloth robe. I wrapped myself up in it and headed quietly downstairs to the kitchen to find some coffee.

The white marble kitchen was filled with the morning sun and a pot of coffee was already warm on the counter. I frowned at it for a moment before remembering that one of the perks of dating a billionaire was the house staff. A quick glance in the fridge showed me a pre-made plate of bagels and lox with all the fixings. A girl could get used to having breakfast made for her.

I found some creamer in the fridge and poured a big cup of coffee. Whoever had made up the breakfast platter had also left the day's weather and sailing report on the kitchen counter. Glancing over it, I knew it was going to be a wonderful day for sailing. The hurricane warnings were far away, and our little island was promised blue skies and a fair wind. Outside the sky was already clear and the waves glistened with opportunity.

I stepped out onto the porch, my fingers wrapped around the coffee mug, and leaned up against the railing. My boat bobbed gently at the end of the dock, and I had to fight the urge to go wake Robbie up so we could take it out. The morning was still young, and we would have plenty of time yet for practice.

"Oh, you must be Mrs. Owen Parker," a voice said. I stood up straight, nearly spilling my coffee over my hands. A handsome man with spiky bleach blonde hair smiled up at me. The collar on his shirt was popped with a pair of oversized aviator sunglasses hanging from the collar. I frowned slightly; this house was supposed to be on a private beach.

"Um, no, actually. I'm not Mrs. Parker," I replied, feeling a bit flustered and annoyed. I set my cup on the railing and made sure the robe was securely tied around my waist.

The man's face twisted into what should have passed for a smile, but his eyes lingered just a little too long at my robe. I resisted the urge to tighten it further.

"Well, in that case, forget I said anything about a wife," he said. His blue eyes leered up at me and I fought the urge to just go inside. This was my porch, and I was allowed to be out drinking coffee in a robe and not be ogled.

"Can I help you with something?" I finally asked as he continued to look at me as though I were something he could buy. My peaceful cup of coffee out on the deck was turning into a blood-pressure raising experience.

"I'm Thomas Grant, a friend of Owen's. Is he around by chance?" He glanced around as though Owen might appear at any moment.

"No, I'm afraid he's not." I was trying very hard to remember my manners. If this man really did know Owen, then he was most likely very wealthy and would have connections. I didn't want to endanger any of Owen's business dealings by being rude while staying at his house. "We're friends of his and he's letting us use the house for the week."

The man nodded and unclasped the aviator glasses from his shirt and slid them over his eyes. "That explains the boat, then. Owen is a decent sailor, but he prefers something a little more classy than *that*."

I nearly flung my coffee at his head. "*That* is my boat."

Grant tipped his head forward, and he peered over his sunglasses at me. "My apologies." He flashed me a very fake smile full of perfect teeth. "Be careful on her. She looks like more boat than you're ready for."

My hand balled into a fist, and my nails bit into the flesh. I wanted to punch him and that smug look off his face; instead, I put on my sweetest smile. "I'm sorry. I don't think I introduced myself. I'm Samantha Conners, winner of the 2012 Spring Sailing Championship. I don't remember asking your opinion on the boat, but I think I'll be okay. Thanks."

Grant crossed his arms, glancing back over his shoulder at my boat, and then shrugged. "Again, I apologize." There was no sincerity to his voice though. "I suppose from here you just don't look like much of a sailor."

Gee, was it my pajamas that gave you that impression? I wondered if the local authorities would arrest me for murder or give me a public service medal if I murdered him right there. I couldn't be the only person on the island that he managed to insult. My fist clenched just a little more tightly as I forced out a polite smile. "It was very nice to meet you, Mr. Grant, but I'm afraid I am out of coffee. Have a wonderful day."

I turned on my heel, seething inwardly and nearly sloshing my half-full coffee cup all over the porch. I slammed the glass door, glad to see him already half way down the beach. I kept watching him until he was past my boat, hoping that he would trip and eat a mouthful of sand.

"What's with the scowl?" Robbie asked, kissing my cheek gently. I had been so intent on watching the annoying man leave that I didn't hear him come up behind me.

"You ever hear of someone called Thomas Grant?" I picked up my coffee cup and went to refill it. Hopefully, the second cup would end up smoother than the first.

Robbie's face twisted with dislike as he glanced out the window. "Yeah, I've heard of him." He shook his head as though something bitter was in his mouth. "Meeting him would explain the scowl. How'd you manage to run into him in your bathrobe?"

"I stepped outside to enjoy the sun when he decided to insult my boat." I set my coffee cup down hard on the kitchen counter.

"That man is a class A jerk. I've raced him a couple of times." Robbie caught me in the kitchen and put his hands on my shoulders. "He's good, but he's arrogant and I'm pretty sure he has a whole tree stuck up his ass."

I giggled at the image in my head and Robbie smiled.

"Don't you worry about him or his insults," Robbie said, leaning forward to kiss my forehead softly and soothe away the vexation. "We're here to practice for the race, not to worry about some snotty jackass who trespasses on private property."

I nodded and snuggled up to his chest. "You're right. Let's eat and get out on the water. It's a beautiful day."

Robbie wrapped his arms around me and squeezed, hugging the annoyance right out of me. I wasn't about to let Thomas Grant ruin my day. I had too much to look forward to.

CHAPTER 15

I released the sheet, letting it fall back into the starting position for what felt like the millionth time. Robbie and I were doing drills to prepare for the Invitational, and the best way to get good and fast at something was to do it a billion times.

"You ready for a break?" Robbie called out as I lowered the jib sail to prepare for yet another drill. I nodded eagerly, glad to have a little break from practicing. I felt like we were making real progress in our teamwork and sailing. Despite the hard work, I was having a good time.

Robbie turned the boat into the wind, and I lowered the mainsail so that we would just float out on the open ocean. Several other white sails bobbed within sight of the island, but they were far enough away that it felt like we had the entire ocean to ourselves.

Together, we sat on the bow of the ship. The sky was bright blue and the clouds seemed too perfect to be real. Sunlight glimmered off of the faceted waves, sparkling into eternity. Everything was so beautiful.

"Here you go," Robbie said, handing me a Snickers candy

bar. I grinned, turning the candy over in my hands. He already had stripped the wrapper from his and taken two large bites by the time I even got a nibble on mine.

Smiling, I shook my head at him. "You are so like your dad. He loved his candy, too."

Robbie froze and then swallowed hard. "I am nothing like my father."

The vehemence in his voice surprised me. I remembered Daniel Saunders as a driven man, always trying to excel at business and give his children a better life. The idea that Robbie was so against being like him surprised me.

"I remember your dad fondly. He was always nice to me. Remember how he used to take us sailing in the morning?" I smiled down at the candy in my hand. "He would bring Snickers bars for us."

"So? We stopped sailing, and he stopped caring." Robbie turned away from me, and the temperature on the boat seemed to drop a few degrees.

"That's not true, Robbie, and you know it. He loved you," I said, putting my hand on his shoulder. He stiffened and stared out at the open ocean.

"You say that, but you weren't there." His voice was low and soft. There was so much pain in it that I just wanted to wrap my arms around him and take all the hurt away.

"He gave you his candy bar. That's how I know he loved you," I said. Robbie turned, his brows pinched and confused.

"What are you talking about?"

"Do you remember how your dad used to take us out sailing, and before we left, he would give us each a candy bar? It was always a Snickers," I said, gesturing to the candy in my hand. Robbie nodded.

"I remember. Mom said they weren't good for us, so she

never let us have them. They were a special treat, and we'd always sit on the deck and eat them."

"Do you remember the time yours went overboard?" I asked.

"You mean the time *someone* knocked it out of my hand, and it went spiraling into the water and crushed my soul?" Robbie asked, raising his eyebrows and giving me a pointed look.

"That's not the important part of the story. The important part was that you were whining about it-" I started.

"I was not whining!" Robbie interjected.

"The important part is that you were crushed," I said before he could interrupt again. "It was a special thing, and you didn't have yours anymore. I remember your dad looked out at the bar floating away, reached into his jacket pocket and just handed you his." I looked up at Robbie and shrugged. "The whole reason we even got them was because your dad loved his Snickers, and your mom wouldn't let him have any. But he didn't even pause for a second; he just gave it to you because he wanted you to be happy."

Robbie sat there quietly. He frowned, remembering the event. I didn't think he had ever looked at it that way before.

"I know a Snickers bar isn't much, but it was just the way that he did it. When he handed it to you, there was no remorse on his face. It was joy that he was going to make you smile. I remember the expression because it was such an expression of fatherly love that it's etched into my memory." I paused and took his hand. "I know you didn't see it then, but he loved you. A lot."

Robbie was silent, his green eyes searching the waves as if they could reveal some sort of answer. The words came out slowly as he said, "I had forgotten that."

He looked up at me and then shook his head. "But that

was before. As I got older, it was always about the company with him. How I should be involved and do stuff with it. Always."

"Robbie, that company was his life. He and your mom poured their blood, sweat, and tears into that company. It was like their child. And I know you hated it, but can you imagine how much it hurt them when you wanted nothing to do with it? It would be like your son not wanting to sail." I stepped up close to him, tipping my face up under his so he had to look at me. "I'm not saying they were right, but it wasn't just that they were harping on you."

Robbie sighed, turning his head away from me. I knew he didn't like being told he was wrong, but to see his heartache over his father's perceived dislike of him was something I couldn't bear. I had to do something to stop it.

"The company was his life. I tried, but I just never understood what was so interesting about oil and accounting. No wonder he loved Jack more," Robbie said sullenly.

I put my fingers on his cheek, turning his head back to look at me. "Jack casts a big shadow, and it's hard to get out from under it. You got the unlucky casting of the second son." I smiled gently at him. "But Robbie, just because your brother and your father bonded over the company, and you didn't, doesn't mean he didn't love you any less. He gave you his candy bar."

Robbie pulled away from my gaze, blinking away tears. I could practically hear the thoughts buzzing through his head as he reevaluated his memories and tried to look at his father as just a man. It was difficult not to see his father as the god that all children see their parents as, but he was trying.

"You aren't your father Robbie. But you are his son. I see the best parts of him in you. The same unstoppable drive and desire to succeed." I put my hand on his shoulder again, and he sat very still under my fingers, staring out at the water. "You never give up and neither did he, you just have different passions. His was his business; yours is sailing. Your passion drives you, and sometimes it blinds you to the things around you. His did. He still loved you, he just got wrapped up in the company and forgot to look around."

He turned slowly, his green eyes full of emotion. There was a depth to him that I loved. His hand found my cheek, his fingers soft and gentle. "I'm looking around now. And I see you."

I smiled under his hand, leaning forward to kiss him. Our lips touched for only a moment, but it was full of tender emotion.

"I love you, Sam. I think I always have. You bring out the best in me, and you help me to see clearly. I don't know what I would do without you." His fingers caressed my cheek and then tucked a strand of hair behind my ear. Our eyes were locked, and I was lost in his green depths, swimming away on his love.

"I love you too, Robbie," I whispered. His fingers dropped to my chin, guiding my mouth to his. I could taste the candy on his tongue. My heart sang in my chest because Robbie loved me. And I loved him. There was nothing that could ruin this moment.

"So this is what champions do to practice?" A voice called out across the water.

Robbie stiffened and we both fell back, glancing about to discover the owner of the voice. On our port side a beautiful and very expensive racing yacht labeled *The Gauntlet* was pulling up next to us. Thomas Grant was at the wheel, a smirk twisting his lips under oversized sunglasses.

I scrambled to my feet, wiping away the kiss with the

back of my hand. I wished the blush would fade, but I knew I was beet red. Robbie gave a wooden smile, raising his hand in a welcoming gesture.

"Hello, Thomas." Robbie's voice was monotone.

"Robbie! I hear you're entered in the Champion of Champions race? Good luck. Sarah here's won it three years running. We're looking to make it four." Grant sneered and motioned to a stunning young woman handling the ropes of *The Gauntlet's* gray sails. She was model perfect with dark hair, olive skin, and intense brown eyes. I recognized her immediately as Sarah Parish, one of my biggest sailing inspirations.

"Good luck to you with that," Robbie called back. He sauntered to the railing, leaning over to peer into the water. "*The Gauntlet*, eh? She appears to be listing a little to the starboard."

"What?" Grant frowned and then regained his composure. "I'm sure it's nothing. Since we've happened to run into you out here, I was wondering if you'd be interested in a friendly race? You know, as practice for the big day coming up?"

Robbie and I glanced at one another and I grinned. I was tired of drills; a race would be perfect practice. Plus I wanted to drive him into the sandy bottom of the ocean and bury those stupid sunglasses.

"That sounds like fun," Robbie answered with a grin. I rubbed my hands together; adrenaline was already starting to creep into my system. I lived for racing.

"First one to Blue Cove Harbor. Start at Shark Tooth Rock, round the buoy, and into the harbor. Normal rules." Grant gave a mirthless smirk that made me feel a little sick to my stomach. "I can't wait to see what the competition for the race is going to be like."

Robbie and I turned toward one another and grinned. We were going to make him eat our bubbles.

~

We maneuvered the two boats toward Shark Tooth Rock. A jagged piece of gray granite reared out of the water, looking very much like a giant shark had left a tooth pointing to the sky. I had the jib up, the wind crackling through the sail as we coaxed our boat to a strong starting speed. Robbie and Grant exchanged nods as they both crossed the imaginary starting line emanating from the rock. I grinned. The race was on.

The buoy was upwind, so we began a series of tacks. *The Gauntlet* and *Avery's Hope* crisscrossed paths as we each zigzagged at 45 degree angles to the wind, allowing us to sail "against" the wind. Each turn required us to change the sheet positions, controlling the sails in unison. If we didn't do them properly, or in sync, we would fall behind.

The sails crackled like strange clouds, and water sprayed up into the air, shimmering like diamonds as it landed on the boat. My feet thudded against the deck as I hurried to and fro, adjusting sheets and following Robbie's commands. I loved this part of the race; the part where anything was possible and the world was nothing but wind and waves.

"He's coming in on the starboard tack," Robbie called out. "We're going to go to port."

"Got it, Skipper!" I yelled, running to the jib sheets and positioning them to tack. The wind blew my hair into my eyes, but I didn't let go of the lines, concentrating solely on my task. We needed to turn to catch the wind in the other direction.

"I need more helm!" Robbie yelled with frustration as

the boat started to slow as we lost the wind. "We're not on our angle!"

I grunted as I pulled the sheet in. I could hear Grant and Sarah calling out to one another almost as if they were singing a duet as they pulled on ropes and scampered around the deck.

Grant fell behind us slightly, and I grinned until I realized what he was doing. As I started to work the jib sail in order to tack again, he went slightly to the side of our boat, forcing us to continue straight instead of zigzagging. He was going to force us off path and make us work that much harder to come back.

Robbie snarled with frustration as he attempted to tack again, but found Grant's boat directly in his path. He frowned and shouted out an order to fix the mainsail, and I hopped to the sheet, pulling and winching the sail into a different position. We had to change our position, or we would sail past the buoy and miss the turn.

We slowed slightly and overlapped his boat with ours.

I could hear Grant curse as we took the wind out of his sails, our own sails catching the breeze before it could power his. Grant called with authority to Sarah, and she called back as they worked to free themselves from our overlap. The buoy was coming up fast, and I began to pull the jib. Robbie yelled that it was too early, but the damage was done.

As we rounded the turning mark, Grant sped ahead, free in his own wind again. I growled; the rope slid under my hands as I attempted to maneuver the sail back into the proper position. Robbie yelled a command, thinking I already had the sheet in position; I struggled to finish the maneuver, but I could feel the boat slow again. I cursed again, feeling out of sync with Robbie and the boat.

Grant sped forward.

The Gauntlet had taken control of the race and was dominating. Grant had found a current and was using it in addition to the sails to propel him faster. I could see the two of them in the other boat, performing the maneuvers that I knew we needed to perform, but doing them just seconds faster. Grant and Sarah were a well-oiled team with far more practice working together than Robbie and I had. Every turn, every tack, every shift in the wind they caught and adapted just seconds faster. In a race like this, those seconds added up quickly, and it wasn't long before *The Gauntlet* was well over two boat lengths ahead. It was a death by a thousand cuts as we continued to lose ground.

The race was over. We had lost. I took down the sails as we trailed into the harbor, coming alongside *The Gauntlet*. Grant leaned against the railing of his boat, smugness spilling off him in waves.

"Nice of you two to finally arrive. We were afraid you weren't going to make it." He laughed mockingly. "Well, at least it's nice to know we won't have to worry about you two on race day."

Robbie stiffened at the helm, his body taut with defeat. My hands clenched against the line, wishing I could wrap it around Grant's throat for just a minute. "The race is still a ways away," Robbie growled. "You won't be so lucky then."

Grant waved his hand dismissively. "Keep that positive mindset, Saunders. I'm sure it will make you feel better when you lose next week." He nodded to Sarah, and she turned the helm to steer away. Their gray sails were filled with wind and victory. Grant gave a sloppy salute and winked at me. "Nice boat, Ms. Conners."

My hands shook as I kept them at my sides. Grant's laughter drifted across the water as we bobbed in the harbor and evaluated our loss. I was furious, more at myself than with Grant. We had lost because we weren't as in sync as they were. What was I even thinking, entering into a race as prestigious as the Invitational with only a week's practice?

Robbie scrubbed his hands through his sandy hair, irritation in his every movement. He placed both hands on the railing, closed his eyes, and took a deep, calming breath. I was half afraid he was going to tell me we should just call the whole thing off. We weren't ready.

"We almost had him. We just need more practice." Robbie opened his eyes and looked right at me. "He made mistakes too. Now we know what we're up against. We'll beat him into the lake bottom on race day."

His eyes burned with a green fire that told me he wasn't going to give this up. Robbie Saunders was going to win the Champion of Champions Invitational or die trying. He went to the helm, his every movement full of purpose. We had a lot of work ahead of us until the race, and he wasn't going to let either of us slow down or give up.

"Tacking drill number nine?" I asked, feeling some of his intensity rubbing off on me. We could do this. We were a team, and together, Robbie and I could do anything.

Robbie nodded, and I went to the sails to start the drill. We had work to do.

CHAPTER 16

I stumbled into the bedroom and started stripping. Everything was sore. I didn't know it was even possible for my eyelashes to ache, but somehow they did. All I wanted was to crawl into a hot shower, eat something full of carbs and fat, and crawl into bed with Robbie.

We had been sailing nonstop for three days since losing the race to Thomas Grant. Robbie had taken the loss personally and was determined to get us ready for the Invitational. We had risen before the sun today, stopping our tacking drills only long enough to eat a quick lunch. A storm was beginning to brew. Not a hurricane, but it was bad enough that the sails were tangling and the going was rough. I was grateful he had decided to let us end the day early. I was so tired I was starting to make mistakes.

We still had one more day of practice left on the island before leaving for Chicago for the race. Even though the Invitational was still three days away, I was already nervous. We had improved dramatically in the short time since our race with Grant, but I still wasn't sure if we were ready.

I could hear Robbie dropping his gear on the floor by the staircase and his heavy footsteps thudding up the stairs. A gust of wind hit the window, splattering fat raindrops across the glass. I peeled off my shirt and leggings, hearing the encrusted salt crunch as I dropped them on the floor. I kicked off my remaining clothes, enjoying the freedom of being naked, and pulled open the double doors to the master bath.

I gasped. Rose petals dotted the white marble floor and floated on a sea of iridescent bubbles in the giant bath tub. Steam from the hot bath blurred the reflection of all the candles in the mirror. I stood and stared at the flowers, bath, and candles. It was the most romantic thing I had ever seen.

"Surprise," Robbie said softly, coming up behind me. He draped his arms over my shoulders, pulling me close to him and pressing my bare back into his bare chest. "I thought you could use a little relaxation. We've both been working hard."

"How'd you do this?" I asked, enjoying the way his warm skin felt against mine. I hoped he would join me in the bath.

His chuckle reverberated through my body. "The beauty of having a butler is that not only does he make coffee in the morning, he can also set stuff up like this." He released me and stepped into the bathroom. "Come on! The water's getting cold."

I took a moment to savor the sight of his perfectly sculpted ass as he bent over the tub to check the temperature of the water. The thought of smacking it sent a shiver of delight down my spine. I suddenly wasn't quite so tired and wanted a new kind of soreness.

I slipped past him, my fingernails rubbing up his spine as I stepped into the tub. Robbie's eyes were level with my ass, and I could tell he was admiring me. I sat down, and the water level rose to meet me. When I laid back, Robbie was right there, his hand providing a pillow for me to lean against. I relaxed, snuggling into him.

"Can I get you anything? A book, a cup of tea? Perhaps a rubber ducky?" he asked me.

I looked up at those pretty eyes of his. "I'd rather just have you."

He smiled. "Here? Or in the bath with you?"

I shrugged and scooted forward. He smiled and carefully got in behind me, his legs pushing on the outside of mine. It was a big tub, so there was still plenty of room. His hands went under the water, wrapping around my chest as he leaned against the tub. I lay back as well, using him as a pillow. I closed my eyes, letting the warm water and scented bubbles take my stress away.

I felt him begin to harden behind me as his hands gripped my breasts a little tighter. I giggled and opened my eyes.

"Shhh!" he said. "Close your eyes. If you ignore him, he'll go away."

I writhed against him slightly. "What if I don't want him to go away?"

I felt him moan softly behind me. "What did you have in mind?"

I reached behind me and ran my hand down to his loins. When I touched him, his member responded with a jump. "Wake up," I coaxed.

"If you poke him, he'll get mad!" Robbie said, laughing.

"Poke," I said, prodding him with my finger. "Poke, poke, poke."

I felt him continue to harden and grow behind my back. "Now you've done it," he said.

I laughed and sat up, turning around. The rose petals

and bubbles obscured my view of what was below the surface of the water, but as I came in for a kiss, I could feel how ready he was.

He stood up, dripping water and bubbles. His huge, erect manhood was in complete view now, and I immediately knew I wanted him. He stepped out of the tub.

"Neither of us is going to relax in that tub until we take care of something first." He grabbed two towels from under the vanity and started drying off with one. When he was done, he grabbed the other towel and came back to the bathtub. He extended his hand to help me up, then wrapped me in the towel.

We were close now, just the fluffy fabric separating us. I pressed against him and our lips were almost touching. "What do we have to take care of?" I asked, leading him on.

He smiled. "Our strategy. We need to know what to do in case the motor overheats during the race."

I pulled back and he started to laugh. I gave his muscular chest a soft slap, and he caught me in the towel, wrapping me up and keeping me from making any further attempts. He hugged me tightly, then moved down to kiss me. I could feel how turned on he was, and I wanted him badly. He gave me one last rubdown, getting my exterior as dry as he could while my interior was getting as wet as possible.

The towel dropped, and our two naked bodies once again pressed against each other. Robbie gave me a big bear hug, picking me up and carrying me to the bed. I giggled and held on tight as he sat me down on the bed. He stood before me, his groin right at eye level, and I couldn't help but reach out and grab him.

I looked up at him. "I want you, Robbie."

He smiled down at me, his voice heavy with desire. "I want you even more, Sam."

"Not possible," I countered. Our eyes met again, and he bent to kiss me. Our kisses were fast and furious, full of lust and passion. The tension in my muscles seemed to melt away as Robbie's body massaged mine. I spread my legs, inviting him to enter me. He fumbled in the nightstand, quickly slipping on a condom.

Robbie moved between my legs, and I felt him press against me and push as he accepted my invitation. We moaned together as he immediately drove himself in all the way to the hilt. I felt him move within me as he loosened me up further. A breathless sound of pure pleasure escaped my throat.

"I told you not to provoke him," he said, looking down at me.

I giggled, but my laugh soon turned into a whimper as he began to thrust into me, using his weight to drive his manhood deeper. His powerful arms kept me spread open. His body was still dripping with the bathwater, but I could still tell that he was beginning to sweat as he dove into me again and again.

He lifted my legs up in the air, then pushed them to the side, forcing my legs together. I reached out and held his hand as he plunged into me again, giving me a range of new sensations. I turned my face into the sheet, and I began to writhe as he went faster and faster. My screams of joy must have echoed through the whole house, and I could tell that it also felt fantastic for Robbie.

When I saw his face begin to contort, I knew he wouldn't last much longer. "Yes! Oh yes!" I cried out, nodding my head furiously. With a last heroic push, I felt a warm surge as he found release. His orgasm passed from his body into mine, and we locked eyes as we both undulated in the throes of ecstasy. He continued to grind into me, and I writhed under him.

Then, it was over. He collapsed next to me, smiling lovingly down at me.

"I'm getting back in the bath," I said. "Care to join me?"

"Yep," he said, snuggling deeper into the bed. "In just a minute."

"Okay," I said. I practically whistled as I went back to the bathtub.

Of course, he never joined me. A few moments after I got into the bath, I could hear him snoring. I let him sleep while I stretched out in the tub and played with the bubbles. Between the sex and the hot water, my sore muscles were finally loosening.

After my bath, I found the fluffy robe that he had set out for me by the tub. I tiptoed into the bedroom, hoping to catch him sleeping. Sure enough, Robbie was completely under the covers and passed out.

I got under the blanket next to him. "Robbie," I breathed softly.

No response.

"Robbie..." I whispered again, poking him.

He groaned, then pulled the covers over his face.

"Robbie," I said, sounding like an annoying ten-year-old.

"What?" he said, his voice cracking. I laughed. He sounded just like he had when we were kids.

"What do we do if the engine overheats?" I asked.

Robbie groaned. "Get out the oars and row."

I laughed, then snuggled up next to him. He threw his arm over me and was back to sleep in no time.

His breathing was rhythmic and soothing. Combined with the soft patter of rain on the window, it made a beautiful melody that I knew would guide me to a luxurious sleep. I cuddled deeper into him, soaking up his warmth and confidence. I knew that we were as ready for the race as we could be. We were ready for anything that life might throw our way because we were together. At that moment, I was completely content.

CHAPTER 17

I stepped into the Chicago Yacht Club, feeling a nervous exhilaration rippling through my body. I was here. I was finally, actually here. Robbie guided me gently inside, the two of us heading for the pre-race skippers' meeting. We were to go over the sailing instructions one last time, any potential weather hazards, and any clarifications needed on the rules and regulations of the Invitational. I usually hated these boring meetings, but because this was the Champion of Champions Invitational, I was actually excited to attend.

Robbie pulled out a chair in front of a prettily decorated table near the windows. The meeting wasn't supposed to start for a few minutes yet, so I stared out through the glass at the view. Chicago's skyline rose in the distance, the gray and metallic buildings looking over the undulating waters of Lake Michigan. Yachts of all sizes bobbed gently in the early morning waters, the sun had started its journey into the day and turned the sky into a brilliant scarlet. Thin, hair-like clouds hung from the dimming stars, the wind nipping at the bright red leaves on the trees.

Red skies at night, sailors delight. Red skies at morning, sailors take warning. The old nursery rhyme chanted in my head as Robbie and I sat waiting. The weather report on the news the night before had said a storm was moving in. Robbie had waved it away as nothing more than a windy day, but the red skies gave me pause. I knew it would certainly be discussed.

I glanced over at Robbie and he smiled. I still couldn't believe this was real. This was my dream race, the race that could make my career, and if I did well, get me more sponsors than I would know what to do with. If I did well at this race, then it wouldn't matter that I had missed a season. I would be set to race next summer, and the Olympic trials would be mine for the taking. Robbie was the best thing that could have happened to me. Not only had he gotten my beautiful boat to the lake; he was sailing with me.

I sipped gingerly at my hot coffee, relishing the flavor in my mouth. One of the perks to dating a billionaire was that not only did we fly in on a private jet the night before, we also stayed in the penthouse suite at one of the fanciest hotels in Chicago. I had never slept on a bed that nice, and the coffee in the morning tasted as if it had been picked in Columbia just hours before. Granted, I hadn't slept much, but that was more because I was too excited than because of the quality of the bed. Now that we were up and moving, I was glad for the coffee. I wasn't usually into the finer things in life, but good coffee was something I could definitely get used to.

The nanny just made breakfast. Real breakfast. I want to keep her forever. My phone chirped as the message from Grace came in. I stifled a giggle and showed the message to Robbie.

"I told you she was good," he said, a smug grin illuminating his face. I wanted to kiss him. He had hired a professional nanny to come and help Grace out while I was away. I had met the woman just before Robbie and I got on the plane, and she was the closest thing to a real-life Mary Poppins I had ever met, down to the British accent. Avery was absolutely in love with her from the moment they had met, and insisted on learning how to speak "princess" from her. I was almost sad that I wasn't there to witness it.

"If I could have everyone's attention," a deep voice said from a podium on the edge of the room. It looked as though a wedding had been held in the building the night before, and we were using the tables and chairs. Given how beautiful the building and the view were, it seemed a perfect place for a wedding. I shook my head, clearing out thoughts of weddings. I needed to pay attention.

"Excellent. First off, I'm so glad you are all here. As you know, this is the last race of the season and pits the best sailors of the summer against one another. Congratulations on making it to the elite competition." The man paused and glanced around the room. He was a large man with a wide barrel chest and a thick, black beard.

"First, the details of the race. You will all start here in Chicago and sail to Mackinac Island. The race course is approximately 333 miles and typically takes forty to sixty hours to complete. The record time is less than twenty-four hours." He continued on about how it was a double-handed mixed gender race, but I was more interested in the weather report.

"Now, some of you have already spoken to me this morning, but weather reports call for deteriorating conditions. High winds and an early winter storm are predicted to hit the lake sometime this afternoon. Despite this, it's tradition to race on this weekend, and we're not changing that." The black-bearded man looked around the room.

A sailing team from another table stood and left the room. They were obviously quitting the race due to the mention of weather. The speaker watched them go. "Weather conditions will be difficult for this race, but the committee has deemed it safe enough to race."

I looked over at Robbie, but he sat confidently in his chair, arms crossed as he took in the information. I didn't like storms. As a sailor, I had learned to deal with them, but that didn't mean that I enjoyed them. The most frightening storm I had ever been in was the one I had sailed single-handed into and gotten caught. It was the storm that killed my parents. There had been storms after that, but never one that frightened me as much.

The speaker continued at that point, going over the race course and the rules. These were all things that Robbie and I had gone over before and were, for the most part, fairly standard. I had followed this race every year, and because of that, I knew the course like the back of my hand. I felt like I could sail the entire thing blindfolded.

Out of the corner of my eye, I could see Thomas Grant and his sailing partner laughing at another table. Grant turned, making sure he had my attention, and winked. I felt a blush sear across my cheeks. I hated that man. When the speaker finished, two males sitting at the table next to us stood and greeted Robbie.

"Hello, Robbie," one of the men said. He was thin and lanky while his partner was short and stout.

"Hi, Jackson," Robbie greeted the tall man warmly, shaking his hand. "You going to be our competition?"

"Hell no! I saw that weather report. They're playing it down, but it looks like a real doozy of a storm. It's too late in the season to be taking risks like this." Jackson shook his head, and the stouter man frowned.

"You two are quitting already?" Robbie asked. "I guess Sam and I here will have the race in the bag. You were our only real competition."

The stouter man laughed. "You seriously crazy enough to try and race this storm, Robbie?"

"We aren't going to race this storm, Burt. We are going to beat it," Robbie replied confidently.

The tall man gave me an appreciative look. "Lady, you got yourself a crazy skipper. He's good as gold, but I think there might be a few screws loose if you know what I'm saying."

I laughed. "I think you're just scared of us. That storm's got nothing on us!"

Jackson grinned. "Robbie, I think you finally found a girl as crazy as you are." Everyone laughed.

"Good luck, you two. We've got to go move the boat from the starting area. We'll be cheering for you," Burt said, and the two men smiled politely and left as Robbie settled back into his chair.

A little apprehension started to worm its way into my head, so I made eye contact with Robbie. "You sure we're going to be all right with the storm?"

Robbie reached across the table and took my hand in his.

"Sam, we are going to knock the socks off this competition. You and me? We're a team. This storm isn't going to be as bad as they seem to think it is. We have this." His green eyes sparkled with certainty and I couldn't help but feel a little better. I knew Robbie liked to push boundaries, but if he thought we could sail through the storm, I believed him. We were a team and I knew we could do anything together.

CHAPTER 18

The water was dark blue-green, with white dots of cresting waves scattered across the horizon. The lake stretched out before us, endless like an ocean yet contained. The main sail caught the stiff breeze, pushing us out into the race course at a strong speed. White sails filled the air, crackling and humming as the boat surged against the waves.

Little triangles of boats fanned out across the lake, each boat confident and racing to win. The water undulated beneath us, the wind catching in the sails with a gentle whisper. The sun glinted on the water, reflecting into the sky like a giant sapphire. Despite the warnings for the weather, it was a beautiful, sunny day.

Robbie grinned at me, standing at the wheel, the proud skipper of *Avery's Hope*. His muscles flexed gently under his thin shirt as he turned the wheel slightly, coaxing the *Hope* for more speed. I grinned back, the wind twisting my pony-tail. I wore my lucky racing ball-cap, and my favorite sailing leggings and rash-guard t-shirt. The wind was cold but not unpleasant, and the sunshine was warm upon the deck. The day was off to a wonderful start.

The wind was with us, but it was also with Grant's boat. His gun metal gray sails seemed to be always just in front of us. His taunting laughter danced across the water as he pulled further ahead. Anger boiled in my stomach, and I kept the sails sheeted in tight; even though it was still early in the race and things could easily change, the fact that he was in front of us annoyed me. The dark looks Robbie cast in Grant's direction told me he felt the same.

Clouds began to pepper the sky, slowly growing bigger and darker the farther we sped along the lake. We had sailed all day, the time flying past without incident. The sun gave one last glimmer of red before disappearing below the horizon and from sight. The clouds quickly filled the space where the warm light had once been, and the deck grew cold and gray. I went down into the galley and brought a late dinner back up to Robbie. It was just a simple breakfast-style burrito we had pre-made for the journey: scrambled eggs, spinach, black beans, and cheese all rolled neatly into a whole wheat tortilla. It was tasty and easy to eat, and we munched happily as the dark of evening surrounded us.

Night settled in like a heavy blanket. The water swished gently at the hull, occasionally sending spray into the air. The waves had a bit of strength to them, but the bouncing of the boat came in a gentle rhythm that was almost soothing. It seemed like the weather prediction was going to be wrong.

We sailed silently into the night, the white sails of our competitors like ghosts in the darkness. I could hear their hulls slapping the waves and occasional soft voices calling out speeds or directions. Grant's boat skipped in front of us, dancing just out of our reach. The entire night had a peaceful, dreamlike quality to it. It wasn't long before I checked the time, my watch glowing a florescent blue: 3:27 AM. With Robbie confident at the wheel, I hopped below deck to check our navigation and speed. We were right on course and making decent time.

"Looking good, Skipper," I told Robbie as I came back on deck. I did my best to stifle a yawn, but he smiled gently when he saw it. "We're making good time."

"Good. I can still see a couple of sails ahead of us, but we still have some time yet. Grant's only a little ahead. It's calm up here, and I know you didn't sleep well last night. Go rest your eyes for an hour or two. I'll shout if I need you, but right now, I'm fine." Robbie grinned as I yawned again.

"All right. I'll be back in an hour to give you a break. When we get to the hotel, though, we're sleeping for a week," I said, covering my mouth as a yawn broke into the tail end of my words.

"Among other things," Robbie said, a naughty grin crossing his face. His smile sent shivers of anticipation down my spine and it was hard not to want to have him right there. But we were racing, and I was exhausted. Robbie was right when he said I hadn't slept well the night before. I never did before a race, but the sheer momentousness of this one had pressed down on me. A quick catnap would do me a world of wonders.

I kissed him, relaying my thanks for the nap. His lips pressed to mine and I could feel him smile.

"Go rest," he said softly, and I headed to the hold opening. I glanced back up onto the deck before I went inside, seeing Robbie's strong silhouette calmly guiding us toward victory. I smiled, set an alarm, and curled up on a bunk for a quick nap.

CHAPTER 19

I was awakened before my alarm by being thrown out of the bunk and onto the floor. The boat was sloshing from side to side, and I felt like we were suddenly out in the open ocean instead of an inland lake. The radio hissed a Coast Guard warning.

"...expected 70 mile per hour winds, tornado warnings... high wind advisories in effect..." the pre-recorded voice droned as interference crackled through the speakers. This was not a good time to be out on the water.

I picked up the radio, ready to call in our position, but we were too far out. The lake surrounded us like an ocean, and with the storm, we couldn't call out. We were on our own.

I stumbled to my feet, feeling the boat roll beneath me as I worked my way up the hatch and out onto the deck. Robbie stood tall at the helm, the wind whipping his hair as he kept our course straight. He smiled as he saw me. The sky was dark, but lightning was beginning to flash along the horizon, silhouetting him against the black sky.

Where the sailing had been smooth with only a little bit

of chop, the lake became alive, releasing angry monsters shaped like waves. Lightning flashed in the sky, the clouds finally overtaking us and the waves no longer played gently with our boat. The water was black, tipped with harsh white. Spray crashed over the bow, sending cold droplets scattering across the deck. The sails hummed with tension.

"Robbie! We need to head to shore!" I shouted. "The Coast Guard is putting out weather advisories!"

Lightning flashed in the oncoming clouds, the horizon growing hazy with rain. The last thing I wanted was to be out in a storm. As a sailor, I had come to terms with sailing in hard weather, but that didn't mean I enjoyed it. With the dire warnings of the pre-race meeting, I wasn't looking forward to braving the storm. Bad things happened in storms. Lightning could strike the mast, sails could rip, the boat could capsize, and a sailor could fall overboard into the murky waters. This storm could easily kill us. With the angry skies surrounding our little boat, I thought heading to port was the safest choice.

"No, Sam, we can stay out," Robbie replied calmly. He glanced around at the oncoming storm, confidence filling his face. "We're winning."

I looked out across the water to see at least two boats turning toward shore. Grant was one of them. We were flying past him. I could see the look of dismay on his face as we flew past. We had the wind and were making excellent time. The others were falling back. I bit my lip, worry curling up in the pit of my stomach like a snake. The rumble of thunder echoed off the water.

"Sam, it's just a gale. Think of all the possibilities for your career if we win this?" Robbie adjusted the helm slightly. His brow darkened and he looked dead at me. "I want to win this, Sam. We didn't win last time, but we are going to blow this one out of the water. We are going to humiliate Grant. I can feel it in my bones that this is our race. We just have to take it."

I thought about it for a moment. The stronger winds from the storm could give us the edge, the speed, to leave everyone in our wake. Winning the Invitational would put my sailing career back on the map. I would get sponsors and quit that horrible waitressing job forever. With this race on my resume, I would be able to have my pick of partners and boats. I could make sailing my job, and Avery would have my income and Grace's. I needed this win.

"Okay, Captain. Reef the mainsail?" I asked. Reefing the mainsail would allow us to control the wind better, but it would slow us down.

"No," he said, a devilish smile on his face. "The *Hope* can handle it. Sheet in the jib, and we'll let this wind carry us into the finish line. We'll beat everyone there by a full day."

I nodded, the excitement of winning giving me courage. I hooked into my harness, making sure I was securely tethered to the boat. I didn't want an errant wave plucking me away and casting me into the choppy waters. I was a good swimmer, but there was no way I would survive the storm out there.

I grabbed one of the sheets controlling the angle of the jib, positioning the smaller triangle sail to catch the wind better. *Avery's Hope* lunged forward, skipping across the waves with almost childlike abandon. I laughed, feeling the boat dance as we left our competitors behind.

Rain came up from behind us, hitting the water like tiny stones. I didn't dare let go of the rope as I worked the sail. The wind was gusting and I had to control it. "Robbie!" I called out, feeling the boat begin to tip. I wasn't strong enough to do this on my own. This was why I sailed double-handed.

Robbie engaged the autopilot and rushed toward me, pulling the jib sheet from my hands. He released the rope and pulled. The wind died down for a moment as he worked the sail. For that one minute in time, I thought we were going to beat the storm. The two of us together would come out victorious and we could use the storm to shoot us across the water like a canon.

Lightning flashed, and the wind suddenly puffed in a different direction, filling the sail and pulling Robbie like a marionette on a string. In the bright light of the flash, I watched his arm stretch violently straight and then continue to bend in the wrong direction. Even over the thunder I heard a popping noise. Robbie's eyes went wide, and he dropped the rope, falling to his knees. His scream echoed in my ears.

The sheet that was once in his hands was flapping in the wind like a whip, the sail out of control. I jumped across the deck, water dripping off my cap. My hands knew what to do before my brain did.

I needed to lose the jib. The sail was overpowering the boat, and I couldn't control it without Robbie. Even with Robbie, I would have taken it down. The storm was going to rip the boat apart if I didn't. I let out the sheets, and the jib flapped in the wind like a pennant. The air filled with its clatter, noisy even over the increasing growl of thunder.

I grabbed the sheet that was once Robbie's, and wrapped it around a winch. With more strength than I knew I possessed, I grunted and ground the winch until the jib was neatly rolled up and locked away. It no longer was catching the wind, but we were still moving at a breakneck pace. Now

I regretted not having reefed the mainsail as it sped us dangerously along. There was no way to fix it, though.

Robbie struggled to his feet, his face a mask of pain as he cradled his crooked arm against his body. He was going into shock. He could do nothing to help me now. I tied the ropes in place, watching Robbie carefully pick his way down into the cabin. Fear lurched in my stomach, dread numbing the stinging rain on my skin. He disappeared below deck, and I forced myself to move. If I didn't move, we were going to die out here in the storm.

A wave washed over the deck, the water cold and dark. I had to make sure Robbie was secure and then I had to get us out of trouble. I didn't stop to let myself think. If I thought about what was happening, I would freeze. I would fail. For all intents and purposes, I was sailing single-handed now. In a storm. It was my nightmare come to life.

I left the autopilot engaged, praying that there was nothing to hit in the immediate future, detached my line, and ducked into the cabin. Robbie was curled up on his bunk, his face white as a sheet.

"Hey," I said, taking a lee cloth and gently starting to tie him in. The boat was rocking violently, and I didn't want him to fall out of his bunk and injure himself further.

"I put my arm back, but it doesn't look right," he whispered through clenched teeth. I could see his elbow already beginning to swell. I touched the hand on his injured arm, checking for a pulse. Luckily, his heartbeat throbbed madly into my fingertips.

I turned and opened up the cooler, grabbing a bag of ice and ransacking the kitchen for some painkillers. I fed him four brown pills and tucked the ice up under his elbow. The boat lurched, and I nearly lost my footing. As much as I wanted to stay with him, to make sure he was all right, I had to get back up and keep the boat upright and sailing.

"I'll be back in a little bit to check on you. Just rest. If you need me, holler." I kissed his forehead, unsure if the cold wet was just from the rain. I put on my foul-weather gear, the raincoat and pants making me feel warmer. I hadn't even realized I was cold. Robbie whimpered in his bunk. I knew the pain must be excruciating; I did the only thing I could do, tucking the blanket around him a little bit tighter, and went back up on deck.

The wind nearly bowled me over as I stepped up on deck. I hooked my tether to the ring in the cockpit and closed up the boat. Robbie was going to have a rough trip, but I needed to keep him dry. The thought of him going into shock terrified me, but I had no choice. I had to get us to safety.

I disengaged the autopilot, locking my hands onto the wheel. Spray flew across the deck, splattering cold wet drops across my face. Every wave washed over the boat until it seemed we were more underwater than sailing across it. I focused only on the wheel, guiding us through the storm by the tiny light of the navigation in the cockpit.

I had never seen so much lightning in my life. It was like I was surrounded by strobe lights, each one going off at complete random. Blue light danced between the clouds and purple light seared as it touched the black water. It was like sailing through a flickering haunted house.

The wind screamed through the rigging, drowning out even my own thoughts. I wished it would stop, but I knew I had to keep pushing forward. I screamed back at the sky, venting my fear and frustration in a wordless howl. Fear racked my body, and I clung to the steering wheel in a desperate attempt to keep Robbie and I from drowning.

There was no way we were going to make it. I couldn't sail this boat by myself through this storm. The winds were too powerful and I was too small. I had been forced into sailing alone and now, because of my inabilities, people I cared about were going to suffer. Because I couldn't handle being alone, Avery was going to lose an aunt. Grace was going to lose her sister. I was going to lose Robbie.

It was hopeless. There was no way I could do this.

The last time I had been in a storm like this, the coast guard had saved me. I had been in a tiny dinghy, and the storm had shook me like a rag doll. My mast had snapped in two from the wind, and I was going to drown. I remembered wondering what my parents were going to say at my funeral. Just when all hope seemed lost, and that the waves were going to overtake me, *The Valiant* had appeared. The boom of the coast guard ship, tall and strong, had been like an angel cutting down the walls of hell to save me. I wished for a moment that the beautiful ship could save me once again, and for a moment, I thought I saw it...

Lightning danced across the sky, blue and green and full of venom, but I could have sworn I saw the dark outline of the *Valiant*. I shook my head, trying to clear the water from my eyes. That wasn't possible. There was no way that ship would be here. I had to be hallucinating.

I closed my eyes, and when I opened them, the silhouette was gone. I almost felt more alone than I had before. Panic began to claw its way up my throat, and I wanted to scream and make Robbie come back out. But I knew he couldn't. I had to do this on my own. I looked out at the horizon where I thought I had seen the ship, desperate for it to come back.

The ship never reappeared, but I suddenly remembered something my dad used to say.

Fear is all in your head. Choose to be brave, and you'll have all the courage you need.

It popped into my head, as if he had whispered it in my ear. A strange sort of calm settled across my shoulders, sending a sensation of warmth and confidence surging through me. I could do this. It would be difficult, but I could do this. I had to do this. I had to get Robbie to a doctor. The image of his pale face and clammy skin made me tighten my grip on the wheel. I had to be brave for Robbie.

I smiled at the storm. "I'm not scared of you," I said. I let the wind whip my words up into the sky, and I gave my best devil-may-care grin. If I was going out, they would find me smiling on the bottom of the lake still steering the boat. But I wasn't going out. I was going to win.

The sky was light enough that I could see the rigging against the clouds. The sky was still an angry black, but I could tell the sun had come up. The wheel squirmed like an impatient child and I didn't dare let go of it to check the time. I just had to get there fast enough to help Robbie. It didn't matter what time a clock said it was.

The radio chirped and chattered, the VHF bursting into life. The others were out of the storm or heading for home. Someone had a broken mast. I wished I could pick up the radio and relay my status. I screamed at the radio that my skipper was injured, but without a free hand to press the button, nothing went through. I didn't dare let go of the wheel, even to put it on autopilot. I was using every muscle in my entire body to keep our heading. Every second was a battle to maintain control of the boat.

The shoreline in the distance emerged from the gloom of the rain, thin and almost translucent. I felt like crying for joy. I didn't dare to cry, though. I needed to see clearly; I knew this was the dangerous part, the part where it was easy to forget what I was doing, easy to think I was safe. I was in just as much danger here as I was out on the open water; the land was too far away to help me if I got sloppy.

The wind blew perpendicular into the sails, thankfully coming from just one side. I was reaching along, just making sure the wind didn't switch. I didn't even glance at my speed on the dial. It didn't matter. As long as my sails were pulling me along course, I didn't care. All that mattered was getting to shore as quickly as possible and getting Robbie to a doctor.

The waves had changed their sound. The watery fingers that had threatened my boat, tossing Robbie and me around like driftwood, were calmer here. The rain still fell, but I could see through it now. I wasn't sure if it just wasn't falling as hard, or if I had just grown numb to the stinging power of the droplets. Lightning still flashed, but the thunder no longer shook the sails. The wind was still screaming in the rigging, though, and I was sure I would never be able to hear again after hours of listening to the deafening noise.

I sailed through the breakwater of the marina, turning my sails into the wind as I approached the dock. Since the mainsail was no longer directly catching the wind, it flopped and danced like a fish out of water. I stared at it, barely registering that the racket it was making was dangerous. Men in yellow raincoats pointed toward my sail as I glided into a slip, yelling words I didn't understand. I knew it was English, but my brain was too tired to make out the words.

The boat slid slowly to a stop, and I let go of the wheel. My fingers ached, and I had to struggle to release it. The sail was still flapping and clattering in the wind. I had to tie it down. I could feel myself screaming as I ran to the lines, sheeting the sail so that the men could come aboard.

"MY SKIPPER!" I shouted as I pulled down the sail,

desperate for the men on the dock to save Robbie. I prayed he was still okay. I hadn't been able to check on him, and I was terrified that he might have gone into shock. I needed him to be all right. I needed him to be there when I woke up tomorrow.

Three men tied my boat to the dock, ignoring the rain and the wind as if it didn't exist. I didn't care about the boat. I just wanted them to save Robbie.

I secured the sail, knowing they wouldn't come aboard until it was safe, and as soon as the knot was tied, I was at the hatch. I bounded down the steps, my tears mixing with the rain as I ran to him. *Please, please, please...* I chanted silently. The cabin seemed to stretch out into infinity as I crossed the space to him.

He was still tied in place, his skin cold and clammy. He gave me a weak smile as I pulled violently at the lee cloths holding him in place. The icepack had melted long ago, and I threw the bag of water on the floor. I touched his cheek. His green eyes were glassy and full of pain.

"We've got him now," a kind voice said behind me, pushing me gently out of the way. A burly sailor with a bushy beard and swarthy features picked Robbie up as though he were a child. An ambulance was waiting by the dock, the red and blue lights swirling in the windy rain. I followed the big man carrying Robbie until we reached the ambulance. I needed to go with him, but the doors closed before I could step in.

I dropped to my knees on the asphalt, the rain running in rivers down the street. I didn't care. Robbie was safe. I had succeeded. I knew they would take care of him. Kind hands lifted me from the ground, and I was half carried to a truck. The motor was running, and it was warm inside. I didn't even remember hearing the door shut before I fell asleep.

CHAPTER 20

The room was dark, and I could hear rain on the window. Something had awakened me, but I wasn't sure what, so I sat up slowly in the unfamiliar room. There was a dull pressure behind my left eye; I wondered if going back to sleep would make it go away. I knew it wouldn't, but getting up and finding some medicine seemed like a worse choice than just staying in bed and dealing with the pain. Every muscle of my body ached, and any movement sent tendrils of fire into my limbs. To say that I had overdone it yesterday was an understatement. I had never pushed my body as hard or as fast as I had in that storm.

I knew I needed at least a glass of water and a potty break if I was going to go back to sleep. I coaxed my weak body to sit on the edge of the bed, letting my feet dangle just above the cold, hardwood floor. The room was decorated with a cheerful maritime theme, and I could hear activity in the rooms below. Dark curtains kept whatever sunshine was outside at bay and gave me no concept of time. I remembered someone with strong hands placing me in a car and taking me from dock. There was a blurry memory of someone guiding me to a room and pulling back the covers on the bed before I collapsed and fell into a blissful sleep.

I ran a hand through my hair, feeling twists and tangles all snarled together. I groaned slightly, thinking of how terrible it was going to be to brush it out. Maybe just shaving it off would be easier. I hadn't even changed out of my sailing gear, and I felt dirty and gross. A hot shower suddenly sounded like the most amazing idea in the entire world, followed by medicine, and going back to sleep for a week.

A knock on the door told me what had awakened me in the first place. It was that same gentle rapping that had dragged me from sleep and alerted me to the headache still growing in my skull.

"Come in," I called, but my voice came out hoarse and raspy. I held my hand to my throat, surprised at the sound and the rawness I felt at talking. Just how much had I been screaming? I remembered yelling at Robbie, cursing at the storm, and shrieking for help at the docks, but I didn't think it had been enough to blow my vocal cords.

The door cracked open and a tentative head peeked in. Grace's smile lit up the room as she entered, softly closing the door behind her. She had a tray with food and drink on it that gave a pleasant clink of glass as she set it on the night-stand. I hadn't realized how famished I was until I caught a whiff of toast and eggs. My stomach gave a low growl.

"Sam! I'm glad you're up," Grace said, sitting on the bed and wrapping me up in her arms. I felt a tension relax in my shoulders that I didn't even know was there. Grace was here; she always made sure that things came out right.

"What are you doing here, Grace? I thought you had a test," I whispered. My voice was still too raw to actually speak. Even though I was glad beyond words she was with me, I was still very confused as to why she was here. "Where's Avery? And how's Robbie?"

Grace smoothed my messy hair, a soft smile on her petite features. "Avery is with Robbie downstairs. He's actually in better shape than you right now. As to why we're here, Robbie had the two of us flown out for the weekend as a surprise to greet you at the end of the race. We just got here this morning, actually. "

My head swam with questions, and I couldn't decide which one to pick first. "But you had a test coming up? And what day is it? How long have I been sleeping? And Robbie's okay?"

Grace laughed, a tinkling happy sound. "Here, you eat something and I'll answer all your questions." She handed me the plate of food, and I licked my lips. It smelled so good.

"Shoundsh good," I answered, stuffing my mouth full of eggs. I wasn't sure if it was just ravenous hunger, but they were the most delicious thing I think I have ever eaten. I couldn't get them down fast enough.

"I'll start with yesterday. You and Robbie finished the race just after noon. Twenty-five hours and thirty-three minutes. Not quite the record, but pretty darn close. The storm was just finishing when they dragged you out of your boat, but it was still pretty hairy. We were supposed to fly in that evening, but the airport was closed due to weather. They brought you here to the hotel, and Robbie to the hospital."

She paused, and I nodded, listening intently as I gulped down some orange juice. It was fresh squeezed, and even though it burned a little at my raw throat, it tasted too good to stop.

"That was yesterday after noon. Avery and I flew in this morning, and it is now almost two. The doctor said to make sure you ate something today, so I brought you breakfast even though it's closer to lunch." She grinned at my shocked look.

"It's two? I feel like I could still sleep for another four hours..."

"How about a shower instead? You look awful."

"Thanks, sis. Love you too," I cracked. She stuck out her tongue and took my empty plate. I hadn't realized I had devoured it so quickly. The headache even seemed to be a little better after getting some food in me. "You said Robbie's downstairs with Avery? Is he okay? What about his arm?"

Grace handed me two round pills which I quickly swallowed. She headed to the bathroom, twisting her head over her shoulder as she started the water. "Yes, he's downstairs playing with Avery. She loves those princess dresses he got her and is making him have a tea party with her."

I grinned at the image of him playing with Avery. That man was half child himself, so I had no doubt the two of them were getting along splendidly. "What about his arm?"

I could hear the shower running and I stood up, stretching my stiff muscles and moving slowly toward the water. Grace came back into view, her pretty features in a frown.

"It isn't good, Sam. His elbow dislocated, and it tore a ligament. Given the extent of his injury, the doctor says he's not sure it will heal properly. You did fantastic getting him to care in time, but that kind of injury... it just never sets right." Her blue eyes searched mine, waiting to see my response.

I sat back down on the bed, feeling what little strength I had rush out. I had seen this injury once before. It was in college and it had taken her months to recover. Even then, she never had the strength in that arm and had eventually quit racing. This was the type of injury that ended careers. Even if the ligament healed well, it was going to be at least a multiple month recovery. Robbie would never be able to sail safely single-handed again.

"It's my fault, Grace... I should have told him no when he wanted to ride through the storm. He just wanted to win so badly...for me."

Grace knelt on the floor in front of me, taking my hands in hers and forcing me to look into her eyes. "This is not your fault, Samantha Conners. Even he says it. He told the doctors it was his decision to go into the storm and that you wanted to go to port. He underestimated the storm and it ended up biting him, but this is in no way your fault."

I stayed silent, the guilt in my stomach chewing at my ribs. The idea that Robbie would lose the thing he loved most in this world because he was helping me was the worst part. He hadn't even planned on being in this race until I came along and he volunteered to be my partner.

"Sam, I can see where your thoughts are going. Robbie Saunders made his own choice to sail in this race. He chose to sail with you. He could have gotten you a different partner, but he didn't. He could have chosen to pull the sails and wait out the storm, but he didn't. He was the skipper, and he made the choice to go into it. You just happened to be there." Grace paused and made sure I was listening. "It's a damn good thing you were, too. Anyone else, and that ship would have sank. Instead you made it fly and got him the help that he needed. You probably saved his life."

"I guess." I sighed. The idea that Robbie might never race again was horrible. It didn't matter how fast I had gone; I couldn't have stopped the injury. "When'd they let him out of the hospital?"

"This morning. You were actually in worse shape since

you sailed through the storm and he was below deck. He's still pretty worn out, but the important thing is that he's going to be fine."

Except for his arm, I thought. Grace frowned and pulled me to my feet. "Okay, no more moping. Get in the shower and when you get out, things won't look so bad."

I scowled at her. I wondered if they taught that cheery-get-your-butt-moving smile in nursing school or if she had just always had it. But I shuffled off to the shower like a dutiful patient.

I stepped onto the tile floor, the ceramic smooth against my feet. Steam already coated the mirror and made the little bathroom delightfully warm. Just as I was about to close the door and slither out of my grungy gear, Grace called out, "Oh yeah, I just realized you probably don't know. They said you were pretty out of it when you landed. You two won the race."

My jaw hit the floor. "What?"

Grace came around to stand in the doorway, a proud grin lighting up her features. "Yup. First place. Think about where you want to put the trophy while you wash your hair." And then she closed the door on me.

I stood staring at the white wooden bathroom door, feeling like I had been in a boxing match instead of a storm. Robbie might never sail again, but we had won. Pulling my shirt off over my head made me grimace. It felt like I was pulling off skin with it. Even though we had sailed in freshwater, I was sticky with salt from sweat.

I moved like a robot, taking off the remaining clothes and leaving them in a dirty pile by the door. I didn't even bother to brush my hair before stepping under the spray of the shower. It felt divine, and for a second, I let myself forget everything and just revel in the sensation of being warm, wet, and clean.

I did the conditioner first, finding that Grace had put several bottles in the shower for me. I worked an entire sample-sized bottle of the slippery stuff into my tangled hair, massaging it into every tress to help the knots slide out. I grabbed the brush from the counter and worked from the tips to the roots, the steam filling the small bathroom as I worked. The water cascaded onto my legs and it felt so good to be warm. The simple task of brushing my hair and untangling it, provided a soothing quality to my confused mind.

We had won the race. My sailing career would take off. I would race in the nationals next season. But Robbie wouldn't. He might be able to sail again, but competitive racing would put demands on his elbow that it wouldn't be able to handle.

I ducked my head under the water, rinsing out the conditioner and leaving me with untangled hair. I let the water drum on my head for a moment before reaching for the shampoo. I knew it wasn't my fault, but I still felt guilty. Robbie was my best friend and I knew this would be devastating for him. If I could, I would go back and take that sheet myself. He didn't deserve to have his racing career end like this.

I rinsed the suds from my hair and squeezed another bottle of conditioner into it. The steam was almost hard to see through, but it felt good. After wondering if I would ever feel warm again, it was a pleasant sensation to boil.

"Hey, the city called and they want to make sure there's some water left for the town," Grace called through the door. I wondered just how long I had been standing there, letting the hot water wash away the ache in my muscles as my brain chewed on the problem at hand.

"I'll be out in a minute," I yelled back, dipping my head under the water to rinse my hair one final time.

"I have some clean clothes on the bed. Come downstairs when you're done," Grace said through the door.

I reluctantly hit the faucet for the shower, ending the wonderful spray of hot water. My skin was bright red and hot to the touch, but I didn't care. It felt amazing to be clean. I wrapped a fluffy towel around me and put a towel around my hair as well. I rubbed a spot clean on the mirror with a corner of the towel around my waist; serious, gray eyes stared back at me. What happened to Robbie wasn't my fault. There wasn't anything I could do to change what had come to pass, and there was no way for me to fix it. The only thing I could do to help Robbie would be to support him. To help him with rehab and to help him sail again. I loved him. The gray eyes looking back at me were now happier and less somber. I let the mirror re-fog, and I got ready to go downstairs.

CHAPTER 21

I slipped on a comfy pair of sweats and headed down the stairs. The little bed and breakfast was cozy and warm with a maritime theme. Paintings of ocean scenes and ships decorated the walls, with soft yellow and navy blue accents. I could hear laughter coming from the kitchen so I made my way there.

Avery and Robbie sat drinking tea out of doll-sized teacups at the cozy wooden table. Grace wasn't in the kitchen, but I figured she must be nearby. I leaned against the doorway, watching Robbie play at tea with Avery.

"Would you like some sugar, sir?" Avery asked him, batting her eyelashes as she poured more imaginary tea into his cup.

"Why yes, good miss. I'd love some more," he answered her solemnly. His arm was nestled against his chest in a dark blue sling. Sandy hair brushed the tops of his eyebrows; his green eyes were bright despite his pale skin. My heart ached with happiness to see him sitting there alive and well. I had been terrified that I might lose him.

"Hi, Aunt Sam!" Avery shouted as she set the teapot down. I smiled and pushed off the door-frame, stepping into the room.

"Sam..." Robbie's lips curved into a smile, and he stood reaching his good arm out toward me. I merged into him, feeling his arm wrap around me and pull me to him. His lips were warm and soft, and the stubble on his chin tickled my cheek as he kissed me. I dove into the kiss, my fear of losing him melting away. I had needed that kiss. I had needed it in order to know he was still with me.

"Eww... gross..." Avery made a face, sticking out her tongue and acting like she was going to puke. Robbie laughed, releasing me from the kiss but not his grasp. I loved being pressed up against him, feeling his body strong and solid beneath mine. I kissed him one more time, making a loud lip-smacking noise just to make Avery mad. She rolled her eyes and tried to ignore us by playing with her teacups.

"Are you okay?" I whispered, my arms still wrapped around Robbie's neck. Now that I had him with me, I didn't want to let him go. I put my head on his shoulder, breathing in the scent of him and letting it fill me. It was masculine and clean, with just a hint of salt. "I was so afraid I wasn't going to make it in time."

Robbie nuzzled my cheek, a smile playing across his face. "You made it just fine. And you did it all by yourself."

"Not *all*. You did the first half with me," I said, cuddling further into his shoulder. He felt so strong and safe beneath me.

"Then I'll just take the bottom half of the trophy tonight," he answered. I lifted my head to look at him. A self-depre-cating smile was on his face, but something about it just seemed off. A distance appeared in his eyes. "I guess you can sail single-handed now..."

I gave him a gentle shove on his good shoulder. "No way!"

"You did it yesterday and got first place in one of the most difficult competitions in the world," he said. I shook my head.

"No, I didn't. You were still there."

His green eyes were dark and distant. Storm clouds still lingered there. "Useless and broken in the hold doesn't count as being there." He dropped his arm from my waist and turned away from me.

"Robbie..." I put my hand on his shoulder, pulling him back to face me.

"It's not important." he smiled. "You won. You beat Grant, and that's what matters, right?"

"If you say so," I said, feeling a frown crinkle my forehead. He kissed me softly, and I tried to relax. I decided to change the subject. "Where are you staying? I didn't see your stuff upstairs."

"I have a different room. I didn't want to wake you when I got back from the hospital. It's just down the hall, though yours is bigger. Really, though, I got us the whole inn, so you can have any room you want." He gave me a smile, but it didn't touch his eyes. I wondered if his arm was hurting him.

"It's beautiful. I want to thank you for bringing Avery and Grace. I can't tell you how wonderful it was to wake up and have Grace there." I leaned against him, feeling his arm wrap around me again. "When we were out in the storm, I was sure I was never going to see her again."

"What about me?" Avery chirped up, wiggling between Robbie and me. I laughed and dropped down to my knees to look her in the eye.

"You? Well, I was hoping I wouldn't have to see you..."

She stuck out her tongue at me, but she still let me hug her. She knew I was only playing.

When I released her, she tugged on Robbie's shirt to get his attention. "Uncle Robbie, can I help you get pretty for the ball tonight?"

Confusion flickered across his face and he went to one knee so he would be at her level. "What do you mean, 'pretty?'" he asked.

Avery swished her princess dress as she answered seriously, "Like how the Clock and the Candle help the Beast. Mommy can make Sam pretty, and I can make you pretty!"

Robbie chuckled and gave her a hug. The way the two of them interacted made me smile, and I loved that she already referred to him as "Uncle." Robbie let her go and pushed her hair back behind her ears.

"Thank you for the offer, Avery, but I already have help for this evening." He rose to his feet, one hand still on Avery's small shoulder. "I actually should be going. I have some things I need to do in town before tonight."

"I understand. Are we just meeting up at The Gala then?" I asked.

Robbie nodded. "I'm not sure how long one of my errands is going to take, so I may be a little late. Don't worry, though. I'll make the awards."

He kissed my cheek softly. I wished he didn't have to go. As much as I was looking forward to receiving the trophy, spending the night curled up on the couch with Robbie sounded like a pretty amazing evening as well.

"Bye, my princesses," he called out as he walked out the front door. Avery grinned from ear to ear at being called a princess. I knew he had her completely charmed. Once the door closed, she turned to me, the smile still plastered on her face.

"Well, if I can't be the Candle, then I'll be the Wardrobe. Let's get you pretty for Uncle Robbie!" Avery giggled and grabbed my hand, pulling me up the stairs and back to my room to get ready.

~

Avery clapped as I came down the stairs. I blushed, and she scrambled over, stopping just short of running into me. She put one small finger on my dress, smiling as she touched the fabric.

"You look like a real princess, Aunt Sam," she said. I bent at the knee, the dress flaring out as I knelt to kiss her cheek. She giggled.

I caught my reflection in a mirror down the hall and actually felt like a princess. The straps and bodice of the gown were worked with green crystals in an ivy pattern that caught the light and sparkled every time I moved. Satin, hunter green fabric flared from my hips to the floor, cascading down like a cloth waterfall. The dress to fit me like a glove, and I wondered just how Robbie had managed to get it so perfectly tailored without me actually having gone to a seamstress. I smiled at my reflection, feeling very pretty.

"You need a tiara," Avery decided as she looked me over. She ran to her room and came scurrying back with one in her hands. I hesitated for a moment, afraid that putting the plastic crown in my hair would mess it up, but seeing the look of excitement on her face, I grinned. It was just hair.

Avery very carefully put the crown on top of my head,

and made sure the curls stayed in place. She had "helped" the makeup artist and hairstylist that Robbie had sent over to get me ready. Avery had watched with wide eyes as the hairstylist twisted my hair into an array of cascading curls. When the stylist had finished with mine, she had even given Avery several curls of her own. Avery had then put on her favorite princess dress to match mine.

"Okay, you two stand against the fireplace," Grace told us as she pulled out her camera. Avery and I obediently stood and smiled, posing for the camera. "Perfect. My princesses."

A set of headlights flashed against the windows of the inn, and I peeked out to see the limousine pulling into the driveway. "Time for me to go," I told Grace.

"Mommy, I wanna go." Avery looked up at her mother hopefully. "Look, I'm already in a dress and my hair is all done!"

"It is already past your bedtime, young lady." Grace didn't even glance at Avery as she helped me place a black shawl over my shoulders. Avery pouted, her little lips curling into a deep frown.

"But... I'm not...tired!" Avery yawned. "I wanna go to the princess party."

Grace straightened my shawl and then went to her knees, pulling Avery into her lap. "Sam is Cinderella tonight. We are the fairy godmother. We don't go to the party, but we are very important to the story. You can sleep in your princess costume tonight if you want, though."

Avery pouted for a moment, mulling over the benefits of being the fairy godmother. "Do I get a magic wand?"

Grace nodded. "Yup. And we can sing that silly song all night."

"Okay." Avery turned her small, serious face up toward

me. "Be back by midnight, Aunt Sam, or you'll turn into a pumpkin."

I smiled at her and kissed both of my "fairy godmothers" before heading out into the night. As I stepped into the limo, I could see them both waving at me through the window, haloed in a magical golden light.

CHAPTER 22

The Gala was spectacular. It was like something out of a movie and more elegant than I could have imagined. I had taken the plastic crown from my hair in the car, but there were several women wearing actual diamond tiaras in their hair. This was not only the award ceremony for the Champion of Champions Invitational, but also one of the biggest social events of the year. Everyone was dressed to the nines.

A string quartet played in a corner, and the dance floor was already beginning to fill with women in beautiful dresses and men in tuxes. I watched the dancers as they waltzed around on the black and white checkered floor, the heavy red, velvet curtains not even moving as skirts swished past. I recognized the back of Robbie's head, even though his sandy hair was cut short. I stepped forward, working my way toward him when I noticed his dance partner.

She was beautiful. Not model beautiful, but real-life, girl-next-door beautiful with long dark hair and curves that seemed to stretch into infinity. I wondered how Robbie knew her when he leaned down and kissed her. A hot wave of anger rushed through me until he turned.

It wasn't Robbie, just someone who looked a lot like him. It was Robbie's older brother, Jack. I had met him on several occasions, but he was a full six years older than Robbie and hadn't wanted to hang out with little kids.

The two brothers were built nearly the same: tall with light eyes and soft, sandy brown hair. Robbie had his mother's smile, whereas Jack took more after his father. Still, the family resemblance was strong enough that it had caught me off guard for a moment.

"You think I was kissing someone else?" Robbie's teasing voice whispered from behind my ear. I turned to see him grinning at me. He had gotten his hair cut, but not near as short as Jack's. I swallowed hard, enjoying the look of him in a tux. Years of sailing had him trim and fit, and the tux fit like a second skin. Even with the sling holding his arm, he looked amazing.

"What are Jack and Emma doing here?" I asked back, ignoring his question and hoping I wasn't blushing too badly. He kissed my cheek, being careful not to smudge my makeup.

"They came to celebrate our victory. Winning the biggest private race in the U.S. doesn't happen every day. Rachel and Dean are here too." He grinned. "By the way, you look gorgeous when you're angry."

I stuck out my tongue at him and then glanced around looking for Rachel. I saw her dancing with an attractive, dark-haired man. She laughed and put her head on his shoulder as they spun gently to the music. I noticed that despite the ample room on the dance floor, they didn't stray far from Jack. I turned back to Robbie, touching his good shoulder lightly.

"Are you okay?" I asked him. "You seemed off earlier."

He shrugged. "I had some thinking to do. I'll tell you about it later."

I frowned slightly, opening my mouth to push him further on it; I wanted to know what was going on in his head, but Rachel was suddenly next to me with her hand on my shoulder. The man she was dancing with hung back slightly, his bright blue eyes scanning the room.

"Congratulations, you two!" Rachel exclaimed, pulling me into a hug. She was gorgeous in a cream-colored satin gown, her hair piled up on her head in long, romantic curls. "I'm so proud of you both!"

I felt a blush creep across my face as she let me go. She had always seemed like Robbie's older sister, and hearing she was proud of us was rewarding. She stepped back and gestured to the handsome man she had been dancing with.

"Sam, I don't think you've met Dean," Rachel said with a smile. She looked up at Robbie. "He's my fiancé."

Robbie's eyebrows raised, but he gave her a warm smile before extending his hand to Dean. "Congratulations. You take good care of her, or I'll make sure Jack fires you. I'd say I'd do something about it, but with the arm, I think you'd win." I gave Robbie a confused look and he added, "Dean is Emma's bodyguard."

Dean laughed and released Robbie from the handshake. "I'd be more afraid of what Emma would do to me."

I could tell there was more to that story, but I would just have to ask Robbie about Rachel and Dean later.

"Did I hear my name?" a sweet, female voice piped up. Jack and the lovely woman he had been kissing joined our little circle.

"Dean was just saying how he's afraid of you," Robbie told her with a wink for Dean.

She placed her index fingers together in front of her lips like an evil villain. "Excellent. He should be."

Rachel laughed, and Dean wrapped an arm protectively around her waist. There was more than enough security at The Gala, but he still gave off a hunting cat vibe. I pitied anyone who would try to take him on to get to Rachel or Emma.

Emma turned to me, extending a jeweled wrist. "I don't think we've been properly introduced. I'm Emma, Jack's wife."

I took her hand, surprised at the strength of her handshake. "Sam. It's nice to meet you."

Emma smiled, her pretty features even brighter. "I feel like I've already met you. Robbie won't stop singing your praises."

I could feel the blush creeping up my cheeks again. Robbie took my hand and gave it a squeeze, a smile gracing his features.

"Can I get you a drink, Sam?" Robbie asked quickly, saving me from my blush. I nodded fiercely.

"Yes, please. I'd love one," I answered quickly. I already was nervous about receiving a trophy in front of all these people, and a drink sounded wonderful. Robbie gave my hand a last caress before disappearing off into the crowd.

Emma watched him go, a smile on her face. "Robbie is completely smitten with you, Sam. In the time I've known him, I've never seen him this happy. He's even been getting along with Jack because of it."

"I would have thought pigs would fly before the two of us could have a civil conversation, but he has actually been pleasant to be around," Jack added. "He's even shown some business initiative."

I frowned slightly and exaggerated looking out the closest window. "I don't see any pigs with wings out there..."

The members of our small group laughed.

"I'm actually quite smitten with him too. But I've always gotten along with Jack, so that's nothing new." I grinned at Robbie's older brother and he rolled his eyes at me with a smile.

"You two always were good together," Rachel said, leaning against Dean. "Depending on Robbie's arm, what are you planning to do next racing season?

"Take over the world," Robbie answered, jumping back into the conversation. He handed me a flute of champagne and then wrapped his good arm around my waist. "Despite the arm, I have big plans for us."

I looked up at him, my brows coming together in a silent question, but he just smiled.

"I believe it's time for the awards," he said, changing the subject.

We all turned to face the front of the room where three trophies stood on display. The barrel-chested man with the beard from the skipper's pre-race meeting was tapping on a microphone to gather everyone's attention to the small stage. The lights dimmed as he began speaking, a spotlight focusing the attention of the room to him.

"Welcome, everyone, to the Champions Gala," he boomed out across the room. "Thank you all for coming to this time honored tradition. I won't bore you all with a speech on the history of the race or of this gala because I know you are all here just to have a good time and celebrate the end of an amazing racing season. With that in mind, I'd like to present the winners of the Champion of Champions Invitational with their trophies."

The room grew quiet. He looked out at the audience

with clear eyes, appearing completely at ease with addressing a room of socialites and billionaires.

"This was a difficult race this year. Three vessels capsized, several were severely damaged, and many ended up returning to harbor. As such, the winners circle is small this year." He pulled a small piece of paper from inside his tuxedo jacket and read aloud.

"In third place, with a time of forty-five hours, twenty-seven minutes, and twenty-one seconds is: *Seas the Day*!"

Applause filled the ballroom as two young men sauntered up to the dais to accept a small bronze colored trophy. One of the winners raised it above his head in triumph before walking from the stage. The announcer waited patiently until the applause died down to announce second place.

"In second place, with a time of forty-two hours, thirteen minutes, and forty-seven seconds is: *The Gauntlet*!"

Polite applause sounded as Thomas Grant and the pretty Sarah Parish stepped up on the stage to accept their silver trophy. The lack of enthusiasm from the audience told me that most of the guests felt the same way as I did about Grant. Sarah smiled at everyone in the room, but Grant looked as though he smelled something unpleasant as he took the second place trophy and then stomped off the stage.

Silence filled the room as the announcer again took the spotlight.

"And in first place, with a time of twenty five hours, thirty three minutes, and two seconds: *Avery's Hope*!"

Robbie pushed me toward the stage, holding my hand in his and keeping me from tripping on my pretty green dress. Thunderous applause shook the room as the announcer handed me the giant silver Champion's Cup. Robbie's and my names was inscribed on the base below previous winners. Just seeing my name listed with the top names in sailing my head feel light.

I smiled out at a sea of smiling faces as camera flashes scorched my vision. My face was frozen into a smile, my brain unable to get any other emotion onto my face. My hands were shaking and sweaty trying to hold onto the trophy. I had won races before, but the crowds had never given me this level of attention. I was very glad Robbie was at my side, his shoulder against mine, giving me support.

"Thank you all for attending. Have a wonderful evening, everyone, and good luck for next year!" the announcer cried out over the applause. The lights came back on, but my eyes were still blurry from all the camera flashes. Robbie stepped off the stage and lent me his hand to help me down the stairs so I wouldn't trip on my dress.

Together we posed for several more photos with the Champion's Cup, and then a man with white gloves carefully took it from me to put back up on the display. People seemed to be coming from all directions to congratulate me on my win and tell me how much they were looking forward to seeing me race again in the summer. I felt Robbie's lips caress my head, and then he disappeared behind me, letting me enjoy the attention and glory of winning the Champion of Champions Invitational.

~

I finally broke away from the throng of well-wishers, darting off into a hallway and ducking around the corner. The hallway was cool and open after the warmth of the ballroom, and it felt good to have some space around me that wasn't full of satin gowns and suits.

At the end of a darkened hallway, peering out a window overlooking the lake, was Robbie. His good arm was up against the window, and he cast a fine silhouette with his dark suit and strong lines. Even with the sling on his arm, he looked handsome.

I put my hand on his shoulder and looked out the window, following his gaze. Boats bobbed peacefully in the harbor, a sliver of moon casting silver light across the waves. It was beautiful and serene. He turned and smiled at me, the soft light from an open door catching the green of his eyes.

"Enjoying your moment in the spotlight?" he asked, straightening from the window.

"Yes, but I'd like to have you with me. You won this race just as much as I did."

Robbie turned to face me, wrapping his good arm around my waist and pulling me in to him. His lips grazed my hairline, his voice soft and low.

"It's bittersweet for me in there," he said gently. I looked up questioningly, and he released me and turned back to the window. "The doctor says my arm will never be what it was. The tendon ripped, and he's not sure it's going to heal properly. He says I will probably never sail again like I used to."

I pushed gently at his shoulder to make him face me. "So get another doctor's opinion. This is a small town; there has to be another doctor who can do something."

A smile ghosted across his face as he shook his head. "Jack had this doctor flown in specifically for me. He's the leading specialist in elbow injuries, usually with football quarterbacks, but he knows what he's talking about. It was a bad break, Sam."

"Oh, Robbie..." I whispered. He turned back to the window to stare at the water.

I knew what sailing meant to him. I knew how much he loved to be out on the water by himself, reliant on only his skill and strength. The idea that he might never sail that way again, or even the time it would take to regain that independence, broke my heart. He was a bird with a broken wing, staring at the open sky and wishing he could once again fly.

"It's okay. We won, right? And I can still sail. I just won't be able to use my arm like I used to. I'll adapt." Robbie turned and put his hand on my shoulder, his face serious in the dim light. "I wanted to ask you something, though. Would you still be with me if I could never sail again?"

I put my hands on either side of his face, looking deep into his eyes so he would see the truth in my words. "Yes. I love *you*, Robbie. Not your sailing ability. If it were a choice between you and sailing, you would win every time." I smiled at him. "The reason I fell in love with sailing in the first place is because I got to do it with you. I would love anything as long as I'm with you.

Robbie's eyes sparkled with heartfelt tears like the ocean in the sun. He leaned forward and kissed my lips softly.

"I love you, Samantha Conners. More than you will ever know. I am a lucky man to have you," he whispered, reaching up to caress my cheek.

I leaned into his hand, feeling the hard sailing calluses against my skin. "You're damn right, you are." I took his hand in mine and kissed it, smiling up at him. "I think I'm pretty lucky, though, too."

Robbie's mouth opened in a wide smile, and he gently curled his hand around the back of my neck and pressed his smile against mine. My heart ached with happiness. I was made of moonlight and joy when I was with Robbie.

"Let's get back to the party," Robbie whispered as we

broke apart. "I'd like to dance with you, and since you never let me lead anyway, I think I'll be fine with just one hand."

I laughed and took his hand in mine, the two of us walking away from the dark window and back toward the bright hallway. "You're the one who taught me how to dance in the first place. I only learned the leading part because you taught it to me. You were just too good of a teacher."

The ballroom spilled out light, soft music, and a gentle murmur of laughter. Robbie raised his hand, and I spun in a neat twirl as we stepped through the open doors. Together we waltzed into the ballroom, whirling and dancing as one.

The water splashes against the hull of my boat, a soft, comforting sound. The sky is bright blue without a cloud in sight. I am at peace. This part of the dream is always pleasant. I like this part of the dream. Evan is alive and happy with Grace. Mom and Dad are safe at home, and we are going to have meatloaf for dinner.

I frown. Mom and Dad are not at home. They are in Heaven. So is Evan. I have never had this happen in the dream before. I always lose them.

The wind plays with the sails, the soft, flapping sounds of the canvas merging into a gentle lullaby with the waves. This isn't right either; the wind is usually a hurricane gale that I can't control.

"Come sail with me, Sam." Robbie's voice echoes through my dream, deep and masculine.

I turn to see him sitting in my boat. The breeze ruffles his sandy hair, and his green eyes are as deep as the ocean. He's perfect. He smiles at me, and the world grows brighter. The blue sky is somehow more vivid, and the water is somehow richer.

"Come sail with me," he repeats, his smile brighter than the sun. There are no storms when I'm with Robbie.

I smile back at him, and take the helm. Together we sail into the horizon on calm waters.

CHAPTER 23

he October sun was warm on my skin, complimented by a cool breeze coming in off the lake. It felt good to be on *Avery's Hope*, even if I was still docked. The gulls cried overhead and the boat bumped occasionally against the dock, creating a strange harmony that I loved. I checked my watch again, wondering when Robbie was going to get here. He was already ten minutes late, but I figured he had just gotten stuck talking business with Jack.

I frowned, going over the sails once again just for something to do. Robbie had hired a local to clean up the boat after the storm since neither one of us had been in any condition to do it. The entire cabin had been strewn with food, clothing, charts, and gear; the local had cleaned the inside and put the sails and sheets back in order on deck. The cabin still smelled slightly damp, but it had mostly dried out after the storm. Robbie and I had wanted to take the Hope out one last time before shipping it back to Winchester, just to make sure that everything was in order.

My watch said he was now fifteen minutes late, and I

didn't have a phone message, so I decided to just take the boat out and check it myself. There was no reason I couldn't do it alone, and it would be a nice surprise for Robbie not to have to worry about it.

I untied the boat and turned on the motor, taking the helm and heading into the breeze. Soft white clouds floated on the clear blue sky as *Avery's Hope* cut through the green water scattered with golden leaves. It was a perfect fall day, and my heart was light when I heard a shout.

I turned to see Robbie waving on the pier. I shook my head. Of course he would show up just as I left. I waved back to him and started to turn the boat around. I was only about a pool length from the shore, but instead of waiting for me to return, Robbie took a running start, dove smoothly into the water, and began swimming to the boat.

I opened my mouth in shock, quickly trying to stop. I worried for a moment about him swimming with his arm in a sling, but he used a lazy side stroke that used his good arm to propel him through the water. As he came around to the back of the boat, I killed the motor and dropped the ladder into the water to let him up. As he hoisted himself onto the deck, I grabbed a couple of towels from below to dry him off.

He shook his head like a dog, sending water droplets flying across the deck, but a leaf still clung to his hair. I laughed and wrapped one of the towels around him, picking the golden leaf from his sandy hair.

"What are you doing?" I asked him, looking him over. "I was coming back to get you!"

He laughed, his eyes full of a boyish light. "I couldn't wait."

Robbie leaned forward, putting his hand under my chin and kissing me soundly. Crystal drops from his hair fell onto my face, his tongue sweet with the freshwater. It reminded me of our first kiss, sweet and warm, and I smiled as he kissed me.

"What is with you? You look like a puppy getting ready to go for a walk!" I giggled as he danced across the deck. His eyes were greener than I had ever seen them, and he moved like he was dancing with joy. He grinned and headed to the wheel.

"I'll show you. Turn on the motor."

His smile was contagious as I revved the engine, making water spurt behind us in a thin stream. An incredibly happy Robbie took the wheel and began navigating to a point further down the beach. He looked almost gallant in the sunshine, the towel hanging off his shoulders like a cape.

I could see a boat, sails still down as it floated gently on the water. It appeared as though there was a party going onboard, with multiple people walking around on the deck. Robbie seemed to be heading toward them.

"Go stand on the bow," he said, grinning like a kid on Christmas.

"Okay..." I answered, not sure what exactly was going on, but trusting him completely. The boat in front of us was now close enough to read the words printed in big, bold letters down the side: R&S SAUNDERS SAILING ACADEMY.

"R and S Saunders? Who is your new partner?" I asked, shading my face with my hand to try and read the words more easily. I heard Robbie turn off the engine, and I turned around to find him down on one knee, a jewelry box open in his hand.

"Hopefully you are. Samantha Conners, will you make me the happiest man alive and be my wife?" His eyes were big as he waited for my response.

"Yes." The word escaped without me even having to think about it. I loved him more than anything. My heart was dancing a happy jig in my chest, and I was smiling so broadly it hurt. "Yes, I will marry you!"

Robbie's face lit up with bliss. He rose in a smooth motion, and our mouths found one another easily. The world was full of so many colors that I could barely see for my joy. He tasted sweeter than honey, the rough stubble of his unshaven cheek against mine making every sense come alive. His lips were warm and inviting, begging me to kiss him for eternity.

"SAY YES, AUNT SAM!" A small voice called out from the other boat. I broke from Robbie's kiss as he laughed, turning to see the other boat come alongside us. Aboard was a very smiley Avery, Grace, Jack, Emma, Rachel, and Dean.

"So that's why you were late," I murmured softly. Robbie nodded.

"She said yes!" Robbie called out, waving at the other boat. A cheer went up from the deck.

I pulled Robbie in for another kiss, eliciting a second cheer from our family.

"So a sailing school, huh?" I asked between kisses.

"I was hoping you'd be my partner for that too." He grinned at me. "The winner of the Champion of Champions Invitational sure would help convince people to come sail with us."

"I still get to race?"

"You now are fully sponsored by R&S Sailing," he answered, kissing the tip of my nose. "You in?"

"With you, I'd do anything. I'm all yours."

He kissed me then, filling my world with freshwater kisses and love.

EPILOGUE

The big yacht sways gently under my feet. It feels strange to be on a boat without sails, but it was the best way to be out on the water for the wedding. The boat is so large, I would never want to sail it alone. I smile. After today, I'll never have to sail alone again.

I check my makeup in the mirror, making sure my veil is still straight. I barely recognize myself in the mirror, I look so beautiful. Robbie is going to be amazed.

Grace takes my hand, a soft smile washing over her pretty features. She adjusts my veil, not really moving it, but making sure that it is absolutely perfect. I love her, and I'm so glad she is here with me for my big day. She and Avery are all the family I have left. But after today, I'll have family again.

"It's time." Grace smiles and pulls me gently to the door. I take one last look at my white dress, the mermaid cut accenting every curve. I still can't believe it's me in the mirror.

We walk to a door where Avery is waiting patiently. She grins from ear to ear as soon as she sees me. "You look pretty, Aunt Sam," she tells me, using her indoor voice for once in her short life.

I smile and bend over carefully, kissing the top of her head. She's wearing a real princess dress today.

"Remember, just like we practiced," Grace advises her daughter. Avery nods smartly, takes a big breath, and steps out into the aisle. I peek around the door to watch her as she takes careful, measured steps and throws her flower petals just so. She stops at the end of each row to turn and smile at the guests.

I can see Robbie from behind the door. He's so handsome. His arm is no longer in the sling, and he holds himself with pride. His sandy hair is falling in his eyes as he looks expectantly at the doorway. He's waiting for me.

"Our turn," Grace whispers, taking my arm in hers. I realize that Avery has made it to the end of the aisle, her small face beaming with pride. Robbie's mother guides her to a seat in the front row, and the little girl waves to her adoring fans as the song changes.

Grace and I step out into the aisle, the slow music coaxing us forward. Robbie and my eyes meet and I lose myself in the depths of his eyes. It seems to take forever to walk to him. Grace has to hold me back at a more sedate rhythm and keep me from simply running to him. I thank her silently for always looking out for me.

I can see my future so close at hand I can almost touch it. I know in my heart that this is exactly where I was always meant to be. I was always Robbie's, and he was always mine.

"Who gives this woman to this man?" the minister asks.

"I do," Grace responds in a clear voice. A ball of tears wells up in the back of my throat. I wish my father and mother could have been there to walk me down the aisle, but I know they would be happy to have Grace take their place.

Grace wraps her arms around me, her lips barely grazing my cheek. Her eyes sparkle with tears, and I know she is happy. "I love you, little sis," she whispers. She shakes slightly as she places my hand in Robbie's and then lets us both go.

Robbie's hand is warm and strong around mine. He isn't shaking or sweating; everything about him was calm and collected. As he helps me up the small step, he whispers, "You are the most beautiful woman I have ever seen in my life." I blush because I know he means it.

The minister starts to talk of the importance of marriage, but I'm no longer paying attention to him. My entire focus is on the man in front of me. My best friend. My past and my future. He smiles at me, and my world shines with happiness.

Robbie promises to love me. He has already promised that, but this is for everyone to hear. The ring is warm against my skin, heated by Robbie's pocket. His hand shakes here, but his eyes are steady.

The minister has me repeat after him, promising to love this man I have already loved my whole life. It is an easy promise and one I know I will be able to keep. I nearly drop his ring, making Robbie smile and laugh. He steadies my hand as I put the ring on his finger, just as he steadies me through life.

I'm trying to remember every detail, but everything is going so fast. Before I know it, the minister is proclaiming us husband and wife. I have been waiting for this moment since I was a small girl. I beam a smile at Robbie as he reaches for me.

This kiss is sweeter than candy. Happiness flows like honey between us, thick and wonderful. For now until the end of my days, I will remember kissing this boy, a bucket rolling at his feet, and the taste of freshwater kisses.

A SPECIAL THANKS TO MARINA MADDIX

Marina Maddix was consulted for all the sailing scenes. I could not have done this without her.

Marina Maddix is a romantic at heart, but hates closing the bedroom door on her readers. Her stories are sweet, with just enough spice to make your mother blush. She lives with her husband and cat near the Pacific Ocean, and loves to hear from her fans.

If you enjoy bad boy billionaires, you might also enjoy:

Vegas Knights

After a passionate public encounter with a mysterious and very sexy biker, big girl Kelly Saunders finds herself on the ride of her life. Her 'Knight on shining armor' -- Rick Knight, billionaire heir to a motorcycle legacy -- whisks her away from her soul-sucking corporate job to Las Vegas, where she finds the road to love is treacherous.

As urgent business matters demand more and more of Rick's attention, Kelly is left to wonder about the future of their relationship. A ruthless betrayal throws her life into turmoil, and a devastating discovery threatens to pull them apart. Is their love just so much Vegas glitter or is it strong enough to survive beyond the dazzling lights of Sin City?

IF YOU LIKED THIS BOOK...

Escape With Me: A Midlife Love Story

"I gave it all up to be happy. I'd give it all up again for you."

They say life begins after 40, but Cassie ain't feelin' it. Divorced and feeling trapped by her job, she wants to let loose for her friend's tropical beach wedding. She decides to let her hair down and get a little unpredictable. That's when she meets a handsome bartender, Wyatt.

Despite a few grey hairs, Wyatt's the liveliest man that Cassie has ever met. She knows that there's got to be more to his life story than just being a bartender, but this is just supposed to be a vacation fling. And after sunny days spent breaking all the rules on the beach together, Cassie realizes that nobody has ever listened to her the way that Wyatt does.

His carefree life is enviable, his kisses are intoxicating, and she can almost imagine a life with him. But all vacations come to an end. And when Cassie invites him to visit her hometown, Wyatt reveals that he can never go back. Not to her town. Not to America. Not to civilization.

Cassie leaves, confused and heartbroken, wondering just who she got herself involved with. Suddenly, her predictable life gets turned upside down when she sees her picture splashed across the Internet. And when the tabloids come looking for the mature woman who found the lost billionaire, she has no idea what to do...

...until he comes back.

Escape With Me: A Midlife Love Story

ABOUT THE AUTHOR

New York Times and USA Today Bestseller Krista Lakes is a thirtysomething who recently rediscovered her passion for writing. She is living happily ever after with her Prince Charming. Her first kid just started preschool and she is happy to welcome her second child into her life, continuing her "Happily Ever After"!

Thank you for supporting an indie author. Anything you can do, whether it be writing a review, or even simply telling a fellow reader that you enjoyed this, helps me out immensely. Thanks!

Krista would love to hear from you! Please contact her at Krista.Lakes@gmail.com or friend her on Facebook!

Further reading:

Bad Boys and Babies
    Family Doctor's Baby
    The Billionaire's Baby Arrangement
    Crime Boss Baby

Kinds of Love
    A Forever Kind of Love
    A Wonderful Kind of Love
    An Endless Kind of Love

Billionaires and Brides
>Yours Completely: A Cinderella Love Story
>Yours Truly: A Cinderella Love Story
>Yours Royally: A Cinderella Love Story

The "Kisses" series
>Saltwater Kisses: A Billionaire Love Story
>Kisses From Jack: The Other Side of Saltwater Kisses
>Rainwater Kisses: A Billionaire Love Story
>Champagne Kisses: A Timeless Love Story
>Freshwater Kisses: A Billionaire Love Story
>Sandcastle Kisses: A Billionaire Love Story
>Hurricane Kisses: A Billionaire Love Story
>Barefoot Kisses: A Billionaire Love Story
>Sunrise Kisses: A Billionaire Love Story
>Waterfall Kisses: A Billionaire Love Story
>Island Kisses: A Billionaire Love Story

Other Novels
>I Choose You: A Secret Billionaire Romance
>His Every Desire: A Billionaire Seduction
>Wolf Six's Salvation: A Shifter Love Story
>Burned: A New Adult Love Story
>Walking on Sunshine: A Sweet Summer Romance
>An American Cinderella: A Royal Love Story
>Mr. Darcy's Kiss: A Contemporary Pride and Prejudice

www.ingramcontent.com/pod-product-compliance
Lightning Source LLC
Chambersburg PA
CBHW050407190726

48284CB00007BB/2466